FALL INTO LOVE

KRISTA LAKES

da

Coffee is the best thing in the entire world and anyone who disagrees can fight me

The rich scent of coffee wraps around me like a warm comforting hug. I take a deep breath in, savoring the smell. My hands are shaking as I let go of the door and step inside the small local coffee shop, but I keep telling myself I'll be fine.

"Should I get a latte before my interview?" I wonder softly to myself. But then I think about having to carry the cup everywhere or spilling coffee all over my interview clothes. Nope. No coffee before the interview, but maybe after.

For now, I will just enjoy the smell.

The café is blissfully quiet. It's not empty, but it's not

packed with customers. School doesn't start for another week, so students aren't crowding the tables yet. There's just a soft hum of conversations and the sound of coffee brewing. Being in a small college town, this place is a local favorite. I'm just glad the breakfast rush is done.

A barista is busy wiping down empty tables near the window and I recognize her. My heart steadies a little bit knowing that I have a friend in the shop today. Sydney looks up from her work and grins at me. I go over to her since I'm still a few minutes early for my interview. There's no line for coffee so I don't feel bad taking Sydney's time.

"Well, you look awful," she tells me cheerfully, standing up tall and putting a hand on her hip. "Although it is pretty early in the morning for you. I thought you might be part vampire the way you avoid the morning sun."

I laugh, feeling my nerves dissipate a little bit. The smell of coffee is helping too.

"I'm nervous," I admit, fiddling with my necklace. It's just a simple silver bird charm on a silver chain, but I've always thought it was lucky. "I really need this job."

Sydney reaches over and squeezes my hand. I realize that I'm shaking with nerves. I've had jobs before, but I really want this one. It's exactly what I need right now and I want it badly.

"I'm sure you'll get it," Sydney whispers conspiratorially, letting go of my hand. "I mean, you're here all the time anyway. I'm sure he'll love you."

"Who am I having the interview with?" I ask curiously, glancing around the coffee shop. There are only customers in the cute chairs and Sydney cleaning tables. "It would definitely be nice to have the interview with Meryiah."

Sydney laughs. "No. Meryiah is the evening assistant manager. She doesn't have hiring abilities or she probably would have already hired you. No, the big boss is actually here today. He likes to do all the interviews himself."

I raise my eyebrows. I haven't met the big boss yet. I know he's the owner of the place, but he seems to work different hours than I do. I'm usually here in the late afternoons and evenings, but he's more of a morning person.

I bite my lip. I had really been hoping it would be Meryiah. That would have been easy. She likes me and was the one who told me about the job in the first place.

"Here's the thing," Sydney says, then glances around and lowers her voice. "The big boss is really strict. He's all business. You understand?"

"You mean I shouldn't start out my interview with a coffee joke?" I tease.

Sydney shakes her head. "I don't think he'd get it."

I play with my necklace. Suddenly, I'm even more nervous than I was before. I usually try to use my happy attitude and terrible puns to make people warm up to me.

"Are you here for the interview?" A deep voice asks from behind me and I freeze.

Sydney's eyes go wide and she quickly goes back to wiping the table with renewed vigor.

I swallow hard and turn around.

And try not to gasp.

The man behind me is tall and he's handsome. He's

what would happen if Clark Kent and Indiana Jones somehow had a love child. Tall, dark hair, piercing brown eyes, strong chin, and a body that says he doesn't skip leg day. Or any day.

He's definitely older than me, but then, most people with real jobs are. I guess his age to be in his early thirties, so out of my league. I'm barely twenty-two and just trying to finish college. We probably aren't even playing the same sport.

"Uh... yes?" I stammer, feeling like a complete idiot. I should be offering my hand or holding out my resume, not gawking like a teenager.

"Is that a question for me? Are you my interviewee or not?" The man crosses his arms, looking me up and down. It's not sexual. It's definitely professional. I hope that my dark gray pencil skirt and white button-up dress shirt look business-y enough. It's the nicest thing I own and I don't have any funds to get real interview worthy clothes.

"I mean, yes, I'm here for the job coffee. I mean job. I mean coffee job. The job where I serve coffee," I stammer, turning more red with every word.

If this man hires me, it will be a miracle.

Still, I keep my chin held high and do the same up and down to the man as he just did to me. Job interviews are about the applicant accepting the position as much as the job accepting the applicant.

At least that's what I tell myself.

"She's not very functional in the mornings," Sydney comes to my aid, swinging her cleaning rag and flashing the man a disarming smile.

He glances at her, sighs, and then looks back at me. I gulp down the lump in my throat and grin an innocent smile. The man harrumphs, and motions for me to follow him toward the back kitchen.

I give Sydney a *'please-rescue-me'* look, but she only shoos me after the man. With my heart pounding, I follow him. He must be the big boss she was talking about and this is the start to my interview.

Awesome. I wince as we walk. I'm doing a great job of making a good impression.

I follow him obediently through the "Employees Only" door and into the kitchen. It's just a small kitchen full of stainless steel appliances that have seen better days. The bakery across the street delivers all the baked goods, but this room is used for prepping them. There's also huge refrigerators back here for all the milk products. It feels cramped back here and I'm not sure how more than one person could fit in the small space.

The smell of coffee is still thick back here, and now it's mixed with blueberry muffins and chocolate croissants from the bakery. I take a deep breath in through my nose.

I could live in this room. They should make a candle with this scent.

But I need to focus and follow the very attractive boss man to my interview. I can't live in this kitchen if I don't get the job.

And I really need the reliability this job can give me.

I take quick steps to catch up to the handsome man walking in front of me, and I do my best not to ogle his butt. I am not the ogling type, but the man fills out a pair of slacks.

Focus. I remind myself as the big boss pauses in front of a heavy black door at what I assume is the back of the building. I definitely need more coffee this morning.

He glances a look at me over his shoulder, as if trying to decide whether I'm worth his time. I give him my best no-nonsense expression and, seemingly pleased with my efforts, the man opens the wooden door and motions for me to follow him inside.

I gasp. His office is nothing like what I expected.

da

I had expected a utilitarian office, or basically an extra storage area that happened to have a desk in it. That was how my last manager's office had looked. But this office feels different.

While it definitely could be a storage room, it's not decorated as such. The desk dominating the center of the room is a heavy dark wood, and bookshelves fill the walls. There's a rug on the floor and even a heavy dark blue curtain on the window.

It's warm and has a personality to it that I really like. There is still a utilitarian feel, but it's obvious that he's put time and effort into making this place feel comfortable.

"I understand you're applying for the barista position," the man tells me, leaning against the front of his desk.

"I am indeed," I say, offering him my hand to shake. "My name is Ada Jones."

He contemplates shaking my hand, which makes me blush a color typically reserved for berries. Finally, he extends his own arm and gives me a strong, hearty handshake.

His grip is warm and strong and my heart flutters at his touch.

Get yourself under control, I scold myself. *You can't swoon every time a handsome man shakes your hand.*

I like that he didn't hold back with the handshake. Many men shake my hand like I'm a delicate flower that will wither with the lightest of touches. I appreciate that this man treats me like an equal, not a piece of glass.

"The name is Nathaniel Rhodes," he tells me in a calm and collected voice. He motions for me to sit in an over-stuffed crushed velvet armchair in front of his desk.

"Thank you, Mr. Rhodes," I reply. I take a seat, sitting on the edge of the chair. This skirt is not easy to sit politely in. The last thing I need to do is flash my boss.

He moves around the desk, taking his own seat behind the polished wood.

"Please, call me Nate." He smiles and I can't help that my heart pitter patters. That smile is drop dead gorgeous. I tell myself that he's probably married to a supermodel with a dozen kids.

"Thank you, Nate," I say in a small voice. I clasp my hands in my lap.

"So, Ada," he continues, shuffling some papers on his desk.

My eyes search for a ring on his hand and come up

empty. Nothing. Maybe he's not taken, after all... Or his girlfriend is a very, very lucky woman.

"What makes you want a job at Perk Me Up?" he asks in a deliciously deep voice that reminds me of dark, molten chocolate.

Good grief, why does everything about this man have me interested? I need to get a grip. He's my potential boss, not a hot guy I have any chance with. Not to mention the age difference.

"Well, I've been coming here for a couple of years now," I admit with a smile. "My study group meets here at the café. We've kind of made it our place - we're here nearly every day."

"Oh, I haven't noticed you before."

I wish the earth would open up and swallow me whole. Of course he hasn't noticed me - why would he? I'm just a nerdy girl in my early twenties. A student like the hundreds of others in this small college town. Someone like Nate wouldn't notice me unless I was on fire.

"Yes, well," I clear my throat. "I really enjoy it here, and when Meryiah said there was a job opening, I knew I wanted to apply. The hours would be perfect."

"Do you have any barista experience, Ada?" Nate asks me, looking over a copy of my resume.

"No. Not really." I force a smile, feeling a little uncomfortable. "Not unless you count watching Sydney make me a latte every afternoon."

Nate marks something down on my resume. I can't see what it is, but I feel like I'm failing a test.

"Hmm." Nate steeples his fingers under his chin,

observing me. His dark eyes make my heart speed up again and I do my best not to squirm under his gaze. "I'll ask again. Why do you want this job?"

"Why do I want this job?" I repeat back, buying time. My throat tightens with sudden nerves. Despite the cool of the air conditioner, I'm sweating.

He nods. "Why should I hire you and not someone with more experience?"

I swallow hard, but I'd practiced this. "I'm a hard worker. I learn fast and I'm good with people. I like coffee and I'm honest."

He nods, but doesn't write anything down.

"And why do you actually need the job?" He looks me up and down. "That's a designer skirt. Why do you even need the money?"

How the hell does he know my skirt is designer? Oh god, he must be gay. That explains it. That's why he's so damn irresistible to me. He's completely unavailable.

Focus! You're not here to flirt with the man. You're here to get a job. Who cares if he's gay? It will make working here that much easier if he's not available. Besides, he's too old for you anyway!

"I need the money for school," I reply. I put my hands in my lap and looked at him straight on. "The skirt was a gift. I'm paying for school by myself. It's my last year."

"Here in town?" he asks, glancing at my resume.

I nod. "I'm studying art."

I wait for the inevitable ridicule. Everyone has an opinion about my studies. My mother hates that I'm not getting a "real" education. My aunt thinks it's a waste of time. The bus driver says I should get something that will actually give me a job and that he's never met anyone who succeeded in art.

"Art? What kind?" There's no ridicule in his voice. There's no mocking. In fact, Nate actually seems interested. His eyes are bright as he watches me from across the desk.

"Photography," I reply. Now he'll ask if he can get family pictures done for cheap. That's what everyone asks.

"Landscape? Journalism?" He frowns, inspecting me. "Wedding?"

"Not wedding." I laugh, feeling a little lighter. "I like conceptual photography. I love capturing an idea and displaying the essence of something in a single photo."

He nods, thinking on my words. To my relief, there's no snide comments about how that will never pay the bills.

"So why do you want to work in a coffee shop?" he asks. "You could just work as a photographer doing family portraits and weddings."

I make a sour face. "I've done that, and it's not my cup of tea." He raises his eyebrows. "It's not bad, it's just not what I enjoy doing. And the hours are irregular. I'm really looking for something steady. The job description said evenings and weekends. That's perfect for me. I want reliability."

"I understand the need for reliability and consistency," he says. I wait for a comment about how that's what this job will require, but instead he surprises me. "I'd love to see some of your art sometime."

My heart speeds up. Is he hitting on me? No, that's not

possible. He just likes art. It's a nice thing to say. That's all. It's an easy and polite thing to say to a photographer.

"Now, for the next part of your interview," Nate says, standing up. "I need you to tell me what you think of our new coffee syrup. I'll be right back."

He gives me a quick smile before exiting the office. I glance around, looking at the space. There's abstract art hanging on the walls. It looks nice, but it's generic. He probably got them at some big box store, but they fill the space well. I glance over to a bookshelf, and a quick glance reveals several of my favorite tomes on his shelves.

He has good taste in books. Unfortunately, there aren't any pictures of people on his shelves. No photos of him and the lucky love of his life visiting Bali. No photos of family either. I frown, finding only a single picture of him with the mountains in the background. It's a local photo. I recognize the mountains and the lake behind him. He's younger, more carefree, and he's giving the camera a million dollar smile that has me grinning back at him.

Too bad he plays for the other team, I remind myself. I sigh and look away from the bookshelves and the picture of him. All the good ones are taken or gay. Funny how I've already gotten over our obvious age difference. Not that it matters anyway.

A moment later, the office door swings in and Nate walks back in. He has one of the coffee shop mugs in his hands and looks like a kid on Christmas.

"It's my best batch yet," he tells me proudly, handing me the steaming mug.

I take the mug, noting the lovely creamy color and inhale the scent. Caramel sweetness hits me and caresses my senses like a lover. I moan slightly, even though I don't mean to. It just smells so good.

I feel the flush on my face and duck my face.

This is a job interview! I remind myself.

I drink with gusto, nearly burning my tongue on the scalding hot liquid. That is only one of my problems, however, as the drink is completely bland. Not even a good coffee taste. There's nothing to warrant the huge smile on Nate's face.

My heart falls. I'm going to crush him and kill my job prospects. I take another sip and wish I hadn't. I hit the syrup part of the drink and there is suddenly too much flavor.

I try to hide my shock and displeasure as best as I can, even though I nearly choke to death on the atrocious, syrupy sweet and almost burnt-tasting caramel.

"It's uh..." I finally manage to get out after a coughing fit. "Interesting..."

Nate gives me such intense hopeful eyes I nearly melt into a puddle on the spot.

"You don't like it?" he asks worriedly, pulling out a notepad and a pen. He poises the pen, ready to write as he looks over at me and waits.

"Um..." My mind blanks. I look down at the coffee that smells like heaven but came from hell. How the heck do I tell him and still get the job?

"Tell me everything that's wrong with it," he demands. "I need to improve my recipe. You're the only person who hasn't spit it out so far. I need your help, well, obviously."

A little bit of relief goes through me. At least he knows it's awful.

I force myself to take another sip, although this time

much, much smaller, and I roll it around in my mouth. It takes everything I have not to gag and spit it out, but then I remember how proud he'd looked handing it to me.

This is my chance to be professional.

"It's too sweet," I finally announce. "The caramel tastes burnt, and not in a good way. It's got an almost plastic flavor to it. It's bringing out all the wrong notes for the coffee. Actually, I can barely taste the coffee."

Nate nods, jotting down notes in his notebook. He's adorable, like an overly-eager student. I bet he was a teacher's pet when he was still in school. Suddenly, he doesn't look quite so much older than me. He looks like he does in the picture on his shelf.

"How would you improve it?" he asks me curiously.

"Well," I begin slowly. "I think you need something to offset that sweet taste. You want something decadent, sultry, not so strong it's almost offensive. Plus, burnt caramel isn't really a good flavor unless you're a five star chef. Your coffee here is really good, so there's no reason to hide it behind overly sweet syrup."

Nate finishes writing in his notebook with a flourish and grins at me so wide I can't help but do the same.

There goes my pitter patter heart again.

"I hope that helps," I add shyly.

"It helps immensely," Nate tells me, setting down his pen and paper. "I'm going to have the best caramel latte in this town this fall. I'm determined to win that Best Coffee Shop award this year. So much depends on it..."

He stops talking, looking surprised that he let that much slip. I keep a bland face, pretending that I didn't hear what he'd just said.

He looks so solemn and serious. A stupid desire to

push a lock of dark hair away from his eyes overtakes me, but I manage to stop myself before I get up and embarrass myself further.

He's out of my league. I need to remember that.

He stands up and comes around the desk, plastering a fake smile on his face. I also stand as this is obviously the end of the interview. We're done.

And I'd told him his coffee concoction sucked. I figure I can kiss this job goodbye. Maybe I can still find something at the school dining area. It'll suck and not be close to home or somewhere I enjoy, but it might pay the bills...

"You have the job." He holds out his hand for a handshake.

I'm so distracted worrying about how I screwed this up, I nearly miss the words.

"Excuse me?" I ask. My jaw drops open as I look at Nate for confirmation.

"You got the job," he repeats. He grins and looks down at his hand, smiling at me to shake it. My hand grasps his, feeling his warmth spread through me. My heart does the little pitter patter thing again at his touch.

"Thank you so much!" I exclaim.

And then, because I'm a stupid idiot who can't control herself, I hug him. I pull his body toward mine and wrap my arms around him. I have to stand on my tiptoes to do it, but there I go. It's completely inappropriate. Wildly so, yet it feels so good.

He's muscular and warm and with my head practically buried in his shoulder, he smells like pine trees and dark coffee, like waking up in a forest. He smells so good I just want to drink him in.

I realize I should let go, so I relax my arms so he can escape. But he holds onto *me*.

His arms tighten, holding me in place, and I swear that he is breathing in the scent of my hair. I hope I smell as intoxicating to him as he does to me.

And then we both realize that it's been far too long for a platonic hug. We spring apart, glancing nervously around the room.

He chuckles nervously and rubs the back of his neck. I wish the movement didn't show off his arm muscles quite so well because now I'm staring at him again.

I laugh nervously.

"Um, thanks?" It comes out as a question.

"Is that a question for me?" He smiles as he says it, an obvious throwback to the beginning of the interview.I blush hard.

"Thanks," I say. I smile at him. Good grief, he's attractive. His dark hair is falling across his brow and his cheeks are slightly flushed.

Or at least, I'm hoping that they are, because heaven knows I'm blushing brighter than the sun.

Again, we stand in that strange silence. If this weren't a job interview, I would think he was going to ask me out or buy me a drink.

"So, um, when do I start?" I ask, trying to break the silence.

"Monday. I'll have Sydney give you a schedule," Nate replies. He looks like he might hold out his hand for another handshake and I really hope he does. I want to touch him again.

"Thank you again, Mr. Rhodes," I repeat. My whole

body is leaning toward him again. I force myself to take a step toward the door.

"Nate," he reminds me, his voice husky and soft. "Please, call me Nate."

Sydney had called him strict, but I think he is sweet. Besides, he is asking me to call him Nate. If he is as bad as Sydney seems to think, I doubt he would have me using his first name.

I grin. "Thanks, Nate. I'll see you on Monday."

CHAPTER 3

Nate

She smells like cinnamon and sugar.

My body still tingles from where she pressed against me. It's been ages since someone has hugged me like that, and I can't seem to stop thinking about it. No matter how much paperwork I throw myself into, I just keep thinking of cinnamon, sugar, and her body pressed against mine.

I have to keep reminding myself that she's younger than me. Probably by about ten years. That makes her practically a baby. I shouldn't even look at her. She doesn't need my complications. She has her whole life ahead of her. She doesn't need my problems.

She doesn't deserve the fate I would give her.

But... she smells so good. And she'd made me smile. I haven't felt like smiling in months, but she had me grinning in moments. I felt good around her.

I play with the pen in my hands, remembering her sweet blush.

Also, it would also be completely inappropriate to ask a coworker out for dinner... right?

I've been turning a blind eye to the fact my employees often date one another, but surely I wouldn't be setting a good example if I dated an employee myself. Besides, there's no saying she likes me back.

Wait, what?

I don't like her. I think she's cute, but that's it.

It's not that she smells like heaven and makes my heart skip. My body remembers her touch even though I barely had time to feel her.

With the thought of her body firmly lodged in my head, I groan inwardly and get back to work. Of course, there is a ton of paperwork I still need to get through. There's always so much to do.

As I pore over the paperwork, my heart starts to swell with worry. Nobody knows the truth around here- and to think I came this close to spilling the beans to none other than my newest barista...

The truth is, Perk Me Up is in trouble.

I'd wanted to open a coffee shop for years. I'd worked in several cafés, managed a few, but I wanted something that was entirely mine. Something that the community would love and cherish as much as I did.

Thus, Perk Me Up. It had been a dream come true.

I went into deep debt to open Perk Me Up. Then my dad got sick. More debt and then more debt piled up. The bank denied me a second loan, so I had to go elsewhere for the money.

I went to a local loan shark.

Now I'm in serious trouble. The only hope I have of saving the coffee shop, my dreams, my family, and everything I've worked so hard for, is for the coffee shop to do well. If we win the Best Coffee Shop award this year, I'll at least be able to pay off the immediate debt. I just need to get out from under the loan shark.

Yet all I've come up with is a coffee syrup that tastes like burnt plastic.

An email pops up on my phone. It's a reminder that my loan is coming due. I hate seeing the numbers. So many zeros. So much interest is accumulating. But I didn't have a choice when I did it. I hate knowing that if this doesn't work, I'll lose the shop. My father...

With a heavy sigh, I push the stack of papers away and rub my temples. I'm tired as hell, my eyes burn and my head pounds with the heavy burden I've been carrying on my shoulders. I need to talk to someone. Badly.

I know it's a bad idea before I even dial her number, but doom and guilt are already pressing down on my shoulders. What's a little bit more?

Uncharacteristically, Katy answers after the first ring.

"Nate?" Her voice is deep and husky. She probably just woke up. It is only nine in the morning. Like my newest barista, Katy's not really a morning person.

"I saw you're in town," I tell her. Silence. I could just hang up now and save myself this pain, but I don't. "I need to see you."

I can't help but know when she's here in town. I see her social media. I see the beautiful places she goes to. And every time she comes back home, I see her and dare to hope it's for longer this time.

It never is. She never stays.

"Alright," she drawls. If she's secretly pleased that I've noticed she was back and came crawling back to her, she doesn't let on. "You want me to come to Perk Me Up?"

"Yes," I tell her, finally exhaling. Doom still hangs heavy around me. "Yes, please come here."

She disconnects the line without saying another thing. I lean back in my comfortable office chair and run my hands through my hair. This isn't going to end well.

Katy is staying at her parents' cabin only a couple of blocks away from here. It's where she stays every time she visits.

It'll only take a few minutes for her to walk the quiet street and cross campus. Everything is located only a couple of blocks from here. It's a small town. The "big city" is only an hour and a half away, but out here, it feels further.

The college is the big draw of our town. It's not a big school, but respected enough. It has a good art program, which is probably why Ada chose it.

Ada.

The way she smiled nervously. The way she played with her necklace. It was a silver bird of some sort. The way she blushed, pinking her cheeks and chest. The adorable way her hair seemed to fall into her eyes every time she looked down at her hands.

Ada will be a great addition to Perk Me Up.

Too bad I can't take her home and make her a great addition to my bed as well.

Not appropriate, I remind myself. Still, I can't seem to get her sweet cinnamon scent out of my mind.

Katy doesn't bother to knock. Why would she? She knows I'm not seeing anyone. She knows she can always come into my life. She knows that she broke my heart by not staying here, but that I would forgive her in an instant if she asked.

So she never knocks.

Katy Sterling looks exactly like an emerging movie star should. All delicate features, dark, luxurious hair and bright blue eyes. Her body is lithe like a dancer. She's ethereal. She's too beautiful to be real.

She stares at me, those electric blue eyes filled with longing. And I remain seated in my chair, returning her gaze with disappointment - knowing that nothing has changed.

"Hello, Katy," I say slowly. The feeling of doom is still settled around me. It's a heavy weight that seems omnipresent in my life these days. Instead of lightening it, Katy makes it feel heavier.

She nods and sits in the chair opposite of me, the one that was occupied by Ada only an hour prior. The simple motion of Katy sitting down across from me rather than coming to my side of the desk tells me nothing has changed between us. It hurts. It hurts like hell.

She's still intent on becoming a celebrity. Still dead-set on winning that Oscar.

And in Katy's life, there is no space for anyone else. She made that plenty clear. She wants to appear single. She's no longer a part of our small town. She's outgrown it. She wants to focus on her career. She can't have anyone that jeopardizes that.

Maybe someday, Katy will meet a man that will make her change her mind.

But I am not that man. And the pain of knowing that never seems to go away

Still, I smile at her and pretend that the doom cloud over my head isn't quite so dark. I pretend that she has the power to make me feel better.

Despite our differences and our troubled past, Katy and I have managed to stay friends over the past few months, ever since our breakup. That is not to say I don't want something more- of course I do. But Katy will push me away every step of the way. And I'm tired of pulling her back.

"What's the matter, Nate?" Katy asks me in a soft voice.

I sigh, getting up from the constraints of my chair. The whole room is closing in on me.

"Frank is pressuring me again," I tell him.

"The loan?" She at least looks angry on my behalf.

I nod.

"He's demanding payments," I explain. "He says the shop is busy enough. He says he wants his money."

"He can't do that," Katy says angrily. "It's a loan-"

"It's Frank," I remind her. "The rules don't apply to him. This isn't a bank loan."

"You know my father could-"

"No." I shake my head vehemently. While Katy's parents know me, her father never took a liking to me. I know they are wealthy. Hell, the "cabin" Katy is staying in is worth more than three houses, but I'm not taking their charity.

"Why don't you explain the situation to him?" Katy asks softly.

"To Frank?" I give a bitter laugh. "He wouldn't care. He'd probably just speed up the timeline. You know he's always wanted this building."

I give her a determined look. She knows all of this. She's probably the only person that actually knows the entire backstory of why I needed the loan. She's the only one I let in, and it's obvious how little good that did me.

"You're digging a hole for yourself, Nate," she tells me, shaking her head. "You need to accept some help."

"I need a miracle," I interrupt her.

Katy's doubtful eyes settle on mine.

"And do you think that's going to happen? In the space of a few months?" she asks.

I don't appreciate her tone. It almost sounds like she's mocking me.

"It has to," I say doggedly. "I'll make sure of it. I have a plan."

"Some new flavor of coffee isn't going to turn the whole coffee shop around, Nate," Katy tells me doubtfully.

"You don't know my plans," I growl. I give her an angry glare. Not because she's wrong, but because she's right. My plans *are* a new flavor of coffee turning the shop around.

She raises her hands in defeat, shaking her head. "Calm down, Nate. I'm not saying it's impossible. But you might have trouble pulling it off."

I don't have much to say to that. After all, she is right. Again. I've been pretty unsuccessful so far.

The memory of Ada trying my failed new recipe for caramel coffee enters my mind, and I can't help but chuckle to myself. Her disgusted expression was definitely... memorable.

It isn't until I feel her hands on my back that I realize Katy has stood up and come up behind me.

Her hands on my shoulders feel calming. Cool.

They're a relief. They feel like home. It's a nice surprise since I'm usually the one to initiate things.

I let her massage my tense nerves, but when she leans in for a kiss, I hesitate.

It's enough to make her pull back with surprise.

I'm always the one initiating this. It's always me doing the pushing. But not today.

"What's wrong?" Katy asks tenderly. She runs a gentle finger down my cheek. "Can't I make you feel better?"

I ponder her question. Can she make me feel better?

She can, for a few moments. For a minute or two, I will lose myself in her touch, in the tenderness of her kiss. Perhaps even an hour, if she lets me take her right here, in my office.

But will that solve anything?

Ada's cute face pops into my mind again.

Sweet, young, innocent Ada, who has no clue she just signed up for a job on a sinking ship. If one of my full-time baristas hadn't suddenly quit on me, there wouldn't even be a job opening, even though we're always busy and the coffee shop rarely has an empty seat.

"I'm sorry, Katy," I say. "I don't think we should be doing this. Not today."

She moves back after an uncomfortable moment passes between us, and I can tell she's offended. She doesn't say a word though, merely picks up her beaten-up leather jacket- which I know is a treasured gift from her father- and heads for the door.

This stupid dance between us, where I pull and Katy pushes. This game that never ends well. This play doesn't have a happy ending.

"I'm sorry," I whisper.

I'm sorry I'm not enough.

I'm sorry you won't bend the rules for me.

I'm sorry I'm doomed.

I'm sorry I'm not the man you need.

I'm sorry you're not the one for me... not today.

She lingers at the door, her hand touching the handle. Katy looks over her shoulder and smiles sadly at me.

"All good things must come to an end," she announces in that overly dramatic way of hers, before stepping out.'

ate

I spend the rest of the day in my office and only emerge hours later, heading into the bustling area of the coffee shop. Sydney is just finishing up her shift.

She gives me a sweet look that is also a little bit curious, and I close up immediately. I'm always this way. Any time there's a chance I could open up to someone, I shove them away. No one needs my problems and I have far too many to share.

Sydney's smile falters and she mumbles a polite goodbye after folding her apron and heading towards the exit with her boyfriend in tow. I feel like growling at her to make her go faster.

"Charming as ever, I see," an amused voice interrupts me, and my smile reappears.

"You're one to judge."

Layla gives me a tight hug. Despite her small size, she's stronger than she looks. She snags the pen from my front pocket and uses it to pin her hair up into a messy bun.

Her get-up today is her usually quirky mess, a pink tutu skirt complete with a white cropped sweater, showing off her navel. She's wearing black tights with Doc Martens and she looks like a deranged ballerina princess.

Layla is my best friend in the world. The sister I never had.

From her ridiculous outfits to the ever-changing waterfall of pastel colored hair- this week it's seafoam green- she's the best friend I could've ever asked for.

She ruffles my hair and I hiss at her with annoyance as she starts taking orders from customers filing through the door. She shouts orders to my other employees, while filling me in about her latest conquest at the same time.

She technically doesn't even work here. She refuses any payment, but she does the work of three baristas. I don't know what I would do without her.

"And then I told him to stuff his engagement ring where the sun don't shine," she tells me triumphantly, presenting a chai latte to an amused customer.

I give the man an apologetic smile, but he just laughs. "Best story I've heard all day. You're something special, Layla."

She's something alright.

With her almost angelic beauty and picture-perfect features, Layla has guys throwing themselves at her. She could've gotten settled down a thousand times.

So far, she's been engaged seven times and turned

down proposal three this week. At least as far as I know. I'm sure she keeps a couple of skeletons in her closet.

She finishes more orders and finally hands off the counter to the actual employee. At least the line is gone now. The shop is peaceful with the soft hum of conversations.

"So," she says with a grin, leaning against the wall by the window, but still within easy reach of the counter should she decide to start pouring coffees again. "Met someone you liked, then?"

"What?" I turn pale. She can't know that. I mean, not that there is anything to know.

She pulls the pen out of her hair and it falls softly around her shoulders. She looks like some sort of mythical fairy, even as she begins to chew on the pen. I'm not going to ask for it back now.

"Oh, Nathaniel," she quips innocently, rolling her eyes. "You're so damn easy to read, even when you try to be a closed book."

"You have ink on your lip," I tell her, tapping my own mouth.

She flutters her eyelashes at me. "Do I?" She then proceeds to make sure there is more ink on her lip.

I hand her a napkin from one of the dispensers. She dabs it on the wrong side of her mouth, purposefully missing the ink.

I roll my eyes at her. We play this game like siblings. Me, the older brother, and her, the annoying younger sister. I grab the napkin and wipe at her face.

Layla giggles, trying to squirm away from my touch, and I grab her waist, holding her close so I can get to work on that stupid ink stain. I can't resist tickling her a little, too.

Damn little sister.

"Ahem."

We both look up guiltily, seeing a gaggle of new customers arrive at the front of the shop. They're headed by a girl with crossed arms and a boyish pixie-cut which doesn't take away from her feminine beauty. Also, she's wearing a pink mini dress the size of a stamp, so there's no doubting she's a girl.

"Oh, hey, Audrey," Layla smiles happily, wrenching free of my grasp. At least the ink is off her face. "You're here early today."

I give her a confused look and Layla rolls her eyes, slapping me on the back.

"She's a regular, you big doofus. Considering the time you spend here, you really don't know anyone," Layla says to me. "How you survive without me is a miracle."

"How you survive at all is a miracle," I retort back. It's not the best comeback, but I wave the inky napkin at her.

Layla just laughs and chats up Audrey. Layla moves behind the counter and starts making coffee drinks by memory. No orders are taken. I remind myself that I should pay more attention to things in the shop than just the paperwork. I look around at the group, trying to make myself remember them.

There's Audrey in her pink minidress, a guy wearing the typical college t-shirt and shorts attire, another girl in a blue shirt...

I sigh. I'm going to have to work on this. They will all change their clothes. I need to remember faces. People. I need to try and make connections. I watch what Layla makes each of them.

Audrey orders an americano with a pump of vanilla. The guy has a mocha latte with extra whip cream. The girl has a hot chocolate , and there, behind Audrey, is a familiar figure. As if on cue, Audrey takes a step back and I see Ada.

Layla is making her a cinnamon cappuccino with a pump of vanilla.

Ada's no longer wearing the designer skirt. I'd only noticed it was designer because Katy wanted one like it last year and it had been her Christmas gift. Now, Ada's wearing a pale purple t-shirt that hugs her curves and short khaki shorts that show off her legs. It's simple, but she looks amazing.

"Uh, hi," she says awkwardly. She's blushing hard and I have to stop myself from going to her. All I want to do is smell her cinnamon scent.

"Hello?" I answer, a question in my tone.

"Is that a question for me?" she asks, flashing me a grin.

My heart picks up a faster beat and I curse myself for developing a crush on this girl.

She's too young.

Too innocent...

Too damn... sweet. And hot.

Definitely so very hot.

"I, uh," Ada continues, playing with her silver bird charm. "I'm kind of always here."

"You mentioned," I reply with a smile.

An awkward silence lays between us, which is interrupted by Audrey handing out drinks. Before they take them to a table, I grin at Ada, unable to resist a quip.

"So, no caramel coffee for you?"

She laughs out loud. "God no, I'm still trying to get that taste off my tongue."

I almost make an inappropriate reply about putting something else on her tongue, but I swallow it down.

"Sorry... I don't mean to be mean," she stammers, mistaking my silence as anger.

"No offense taken," I smile back. "I'll keep working on the formula."

"You do that. I'm sure you'll get it in no time." She smiles at me with such warmth that I feel like I might actually walk into the kitchen and make a perfect cup right this moment.

It feels amazing.

I wink at Ada and watch her walk away with my heart pounding. She trips a little on her way to the table, and I chuckle watching her quickly check if anyone saw her small mishap. I want to run over and hug her.

"So that's her, is it?" Layla interrupts again, reading my mind. As per usual.

"Shut up," I tell her, sliding into my spot on the wall.

"What are you, twelve?" She rolls her eyes and wipes down the counter with a cleaning cloth. "It's totally obvious you have a crush on Ada. She's gonna start working here too, isn't she?"

"How do you know all this stuff?" I demand to know, crossing my arms and glaring at her.

Honestly, it feels like Layla knows the café better than I ever have. I may run all the background stuff, but she's the one who keeps the regulars coming back. I know they love her quirkiness. She remembers everyone's names and orders. She makes this place feel like home.

"I listen. You should try it sometime," she says, tapping her ear with a smile. "So I'll be working with Lover-Girl starting Monday? What does Katy think about your new crush?"

I think back to the scene in my office earlier this morning. The way I pushed Katy away, something I've never done before.

"She doesn't know," I say softly. "Besides, there's nothing to know. And stop putting your nose where it doesn't belong," I finish roughly, regretting my words immediately.

But Layla only raises an eyebrow at me, then shrugs and winks. That's what I love about the woman- she's so damn easy-going. I know I can tell her everything.

And I do.

"He's getting worse," I say in a small voice. I stare out at the café, but I don't really see the street outside.

"Yeah?" Layla puts the cleaning cloth away and comes and leans on the wall next to me. The coffee shop is empty now, save for Ada's group of friends in the corner, and I'm enjoying the solitude, at least for the time being.

"What do the doctors say?" Layla asks softly.

"There's not much they can do," I shrug helplessly.

"Are you gonna go up and visit him?" she asks. She tucks one foot up against the wall, close enough to touch me but not so much that I feel pressured. She's just there for me. Like always.

I stare at the floor. I don't know what to tell her. It's too fucking difficult.

"I don't know. I want to," I admit.

"You should." Layla reaches over and hugs me. I hold her tight, using her friendship as an anchor so I don't drift off into the sea of despair. "You really should."

I can only nod, knowing she is right.

I look over at Ada, and she looks at me. Suddenly she frowns and turns back to her friends, as if trying to ignore me.

Maybe I stared for too long. I should go over there, like Layla says. But I can't do it. I can't make myself go there.

I excuse myself a moment later, heading into the back and inside my office once more. I'm always like this, avoiding feelings whenever I can. It's too fucking painful sometimes, when life throws you a curveball.

I hear Ada laugh and I can't help but look over at her.

And I think I've just been thrown my biggest curveball yet.

da

I kick at a small rock, pushing it down the empty street in front of me. Insects are loud in the trees and there's sweat on the back of my neck from the day's heat. The rock skitters and disappears down a storm drain.

But I barely notice it. My mind is on Nate and Layla.

So she's the lucky girl.

I'd thought there was something between Nate and I, but apparently, it was all in my head. I want to scream at how stupid I'd been giving him that hug. How stupid I'd been thinking that he'd held me longer than necessary or that there could be anything more to it.

I'd spent the whole day thinking of how much I liked Nate. Remembering his smile and the way he'd grinned at me. The way he'd pressed into me and how good it had felt to be in his arms.

I'd imagined working at Perk Me Up with him, the two of us falling in love over coffees. A workplace romance.

But that was just a stupid fantasy.

Layla is one of the reasons I love Perk Me Up. She is bright and quirky, kind and funny, and definitely doesn't care what anyone thinks of her. She wears whatever she wants and says whatever she wants. I want to be like her. I want her confidence.

And now I want her boyfriend.

I don't know how much more proof I need. They're obviously together. You don't get close like that without sharing something deeply intimate.

I turn from the street and climb the rickety wooden stairs to the entrance of my room.I rent a shared second floor apartment a block from campus. Another student lives in the second bedroom and we share a bathroom and kitchen. She's busy with graduate school, so I don't see her except when she's busy cramming for a test. She's nice enough, but we aren't close friends.

It's not much, but it's cheap and close to school.

I spend the rest of the evening pouting in my room. I should technically be getting ready for school to start, but I'm feeling too annoyed to pick up a textbook at the moment. Not even my beloved camera has me wanting to do anything.

I don't know why I'm so crushed. It was just a hug. I need to get over it.

I manage to get some of the things I need done over the course of the weekend. My room is clean, my groceries bought, and my school stuff organized.

I'm ready for Monday and school, but as far as my first

shift is considered... I've been dreading it since the moment I saw Layla and Nate together.

I'm not one of those rare people who identify as a morning person, and though I desperately want to sleep in and have an excuse for being late on my first day of work, I get up bright and early. My usual shift will be in the afternoons and evenings, but this week is training. Thus, the morning and day shift.

I mess around with my breakfast for ages, but I can't get a single bite down my throat. I can't even have my coffee, which is saying something. Caffeine is my lifeblood.

At least I'll be able to get some at work once my nerves settle down.

The walk to Perk Me Up- or I guess work, as I should call it now- is easy and uneventful. It's late summer, so it's cold enough to warrant a jacket in the morning. I know I'll hate carrying it around later, but I shiver as I walk in the dark morning.

Unfortunately, the Earth doesn't open to swallow me whole and I make it to the coffee shop in one piece.

The building is a classic mainstreet style brick building that joins into another classic looking brick building that joins to another, all the way down main street. Big plate glass windows show off the comfortable inside full of tables and chairs. There appears to be a second floor above the place, with much smaller windows covered by curtains. They're probably expensive apartments or office spaces for people who want to work downtown.

I know these buildings are desirable real estate. Despite the fact that the buildings are older, they line Main Street and probably fetch a high rent price.

I enter through the back, just like Sydney told me to, and head to the small employee area. My eyes linger on the door of Nate's office, but there is no sign of life coming from it. Not knowing whether I should be disappointed or relieved, I head to the main area of the coffee shop.

"Ah, Ada. Nice and early."

The voice I've been dreading to hear all weekend greets me. I give Nathaniel a weak smile. He looks even better today, clad in a button-up shirt and dress slacks that look way too good on him. His blazer is slung over a bar stool behind the counter.

"Good morning," I reply miserably.

Nate gives me a quizzical look before smiling in return. I'm sure he's questioning why I'm so unenthusiastic, especially after our interview on Friday, when I'd been nothing but excited about my new position at Perk Me Up.

"Are you ready to get started, Newbie?" he asks with a smile. I hate that I like the way he calls me "Newbie." It feels almost like a pet name.

"Yeah, sure," I smile nervously. "Is Sydney going to show me the ropes?"

"Nope," Nate grins at me. "I'm always here when we get a new hire. I prefer doing it myself, and get to know the people I'm working with a little."

Just great.

I know I'm being unreasonably grumpy, but...

I've apparently developed quite the crush on my boss, and I've barely even started my first shift.

This is a problem, since he obviously has a girlfriend-Layla. I don't want to get in the middle of something, but I can't very well help it... My eyes keep flicking back to Nate, my hands shake when he's around, and my knees feel weak as hell.

"That's nice," I mumble in reply.

If Nate is surprised by my lack of enthusiasm, he doesn't mention it once. Instead, he goes on to show me the ropes of the place, patiently explaining how to make every kind of coffee Perk Me Up serves.

And trust me, there are many. I'm a regular, and I've probably tasted them all.

By the end of the demonstration, I think I've got everything down. Nate finishes by explaining which hours are the most and least busy, and telling me I'm free to read or study when there's a lull in customers. We're right about done when *she* walks in.

Layla.

"Oh, hey!" Nate greets her, his whole face lighting up when she walks in. He kisses her cheek and I look away uncomfortably.

Layla's all smiles when I turn my attention back to her, and there's no denying it. She's stunning, and I know she's sweet as pie as well.

There's no point hating her. She's such a sweetheart.

"I'm excited to be working with you today, Ada," she says enthusiastically.

Today, she is wearing a black and white striped dress with platform heels. She still looks tiny compared to Nate, but they give her a little bit more height. And she looks adorable. Annoyingly so.

"Same," I reply blandly.

Layla doesn't say a word about my behavior, and I'm fully aware I'm being a total brat, but I can't seem to be able to stop myself. I'm glaring daggers at everyone and by the time Nate excuses himself to work on some paperwork in his office, Layla looks worried.

Once he's gone and I've practiced my coffee-making skills by making us both lattes, Layla sits me down at an empty table in the sitting area.

"So you'll find out something about me pretty soon," Layla tells me with that charming little smile of hers. "I'm a nosy little bitch. And I don't let things lie."

Surprised by her brutal honesty, I can't help but laugh at what she's said.

"Okay," I say. "So what is your dose of brutality for the day?"

She gazes at me for a long time.

"You're upset," she finally says, and I frown. "Well, that's too easy. You're upset about something to do with me, though. See how good I am?" She nudges me playfully, and I give her a weak smile.

I guess she notices how on edge I am as she quickly turns somber again.

"So? What's bothering you, new girl?" she asks in a soft voice.

I look up into her bright green eyes. She's so sweet, and I honestly have no reason to dislike her. Layla's never been anything but nice to me, and she's a total sweetheart. I'm just being bitchy and awful.

"I'm a little embarrassed," I admit, reaching for my coffee.

"Oh yeah?" She taps her chin with her pointer finger before taking a sip of her foamy latte. "I got busted masturbating yesterday by my neighbor's dad," she says nonchalantly and I nearly spit out my drink.

"What?" I ask incredulously.

Layla shrugs, grinning mischievously.

"Shit happens," she tells me. "Now that I've told you something embarrassing about me, I think it's your turn."

I laugh out loud, shaking my head. It's impossible to dislike this woman, and I was a fool for acting like a five-year-old child just because I have a crush on Nathaniel.

"Well..." I drawl, feeling shy again. My necklace is in my fingers, sliding back and forth on the chain. "I have an inappropriate crush."

"On Nate?" she urges me on, nursing her mug.

I give her a surprised look. She's acting pretty cool, given that I'm admitting to basically having the hots for her boyfriend.

"Yeah..."

"And? You're worried about Katy?" she gives me a knowing nod, taking another sip of the latte.

"What?" I stare at her, feeling more confused than ever. "Who is Katy?"

"Huh?" Layla stares at me in wonder, then waves her hands around. "Wait, hold up. What's the problem here?"

I fiddle with my necklace again. I can feel the blush heating up my cheeks and I'm incredibly glad there aren't any customers around.

"Well, you're dating him. Isn't it awkward enough this

way?" I say in a strained voice, trying to make things less awkward.

An uncomfortable silence lays upon the table, which is interrupted moments later when Layla bursts out laughing.

"What?" I ask defensively, but she just won't stop.

"That's hilarious!" she finally exclaims, snorting loudly.

Even when she does that, she's adorable. It's not fair. No wonder Nate loves her. I take my mug in my hands sulkily, refusing to look at her.

"Ada," she finally says, making me look back at her. She's grinning wide as she winks at me, her eyes sparkly and framed by thick, doll-like black lashes. "I'm not dating Nate."

She drops the news and my heart kind of sort of soars. Not that I'm willing to admit that, but I'm sure it's written all over my face, anyway.

"W-what?" I ask. "But I saw you two... On Friday, when we came in."

"Saw us what?" Layla asks in confusion.

"You guys were..." I clear my throat awkwardly. "I mean, you looked pretty close, hugging, he was touching your lips..."

"Oh my god, duh," Layla slaps her forehead. "I was chewing on a pen- stupid habit, I know- and I had a huge ink stain on my lip."

"So Nate decided to French it off you?" I tease her.

Layla rolls her eyes and laughs, saying, "Yes, that's exactly it, you big perv. No, ew. I don't like him that way."

"But he likes you," I tell her certainly, making her laugh one more time.

"Are you for real?" Layla asks me. "There is nothing going on with us."

"You definitely fooled me," I mumble, looking down at my coffee.

"No way, José. We had a weird... relationship thing in high school. Dated for two weeks before I dumped him. He crawled after me for two years before it finally dawned on him I wasn't exactly his type. Or rather, he's not my type."

I smile at her story, and she nudges me with her bony elbow, winking. Suddenly, I realize exactly what she's saying. It's not just Nate. It's all men who aren't her type.

"Now you, my friend, while exactly my type, seem to be more exactly his type," she pretend-whispers, and I blush. "So, no more grumpy-face, okay?"

Customers walk in and she has me back to making coffees, but this time with a smile on my face.

They aren't dating.

And I'm his type.

da

My shift is nearing its end, and I'm pleasantly exhausted. I've spent several hours on my feet and am currently very thankful I'm only working a half-shift on my first day, as I'm absolutely beat.

All I've had for food was a freshly-baked pecan brownie for breakfast, shared with Layla during our busiest time of the day, so we pretty much shoved it down our throats. It was delicious, but not nearly enough to sustain a human being.

Now it's lunchtime, and I've just wrapped up everything at the counter and handed my apron to Sydney, who's ecstatic I'll be joining her as a member of Perk Me Up's staff.

My stomach is rumbling, I've had more coffee than I

thought I could handle, and I feel great, even though I haven't seen Nate since this morning. I need to eat something soon or I'll pass out.

"Hey, Newbie," a voice calls out to me that has my heart speeding up.

I turn in the direction of it and grin widely as I see it's Nate calling out for me. I try not to stare. His button up shirt is now rolled at the sleeves, showing off strong arms. He's got the matching jacket to his slacks draped over his arm.

I don't know why, but this man has a strange effect on me... At the same time, I want to impress him and get closer to him, get to know all of his secrets.

"Hey," I reply. "Thanks again for the job. I had a great time working today."

"I see you're in a better mood now?" Nate asks with a raised eyebrow, and I nod.

I made Layla promise she wouldn't tell Nate what I thought when I saw them together, and so far she hasn't said a word to him. Layla says I should tell him, but she's braver than I am.

"I am," I say sheepishly. "I was just a little tired this morning, is all. Mornings are not my best times. Hey..."

I give him a lingering look, playing with my necklace and then looking at the floor. I'm not sure I should ask him, but what the hell. My stomach twists, but I get the words out before I can think too much about them.

"At the risk of being wildly inappropriate, do you want to grab a bite to eat?" I finally manage to blurt. "I'm absolutely starving and I know you've been working all morning too."

"That sounds..." Nate approaches me, standing only a few steps away from me and grinning at me. "Awesome."

I smile in response and grab my bag. It's an old tote bag that I use as a purse. It doesn't look like much, but it holds my travel camera and other things easily and comfortably. I throw my light jacket on. It's too warm for it now, but this morning the light zip-up sweatshirt was perfect. Better to wear it than carry it.

"Come on. I know a really awesome sushi place a few blocks away," I tell him.

Nate follows me out of the coffee shop and out into the late summer sunshine. We leave Sydney behind us, staring at our retreating backs with an incredulous expression.

Once we've rounded the corner, both Nate and I erupt in laughter, realizing we must've shocked her.

"I don't make it a point to hang out with the employees," Nate tells me.

"And I usually prefer to bitch about my boss in private," I wink at him.

He laughs, shaking his head. He is so handsome. The sun shines on his dark hair. For the moment, he looks young and carefree. I find I want to grab his hand and hold it. I want to feel his sun-kissed skin, so I keep my hands busy playing with the bird charm on my necklace.

"I like you, Newbie," he admits. "You've got spunk. That is, when you're not pouting."

He's teasing me about this morning, and this makes me wonder whether Layla actually did tell him about what I imagined in my head...

God. I must seem so young to him. Shame washes over

me. I want to impress him so badly, but I've just been acting like a child. A petulant child. Why in the world would he want to do anything with me? He's probably just going to lunch with me to mentor me big brother style.

But before I can ask him why he's coming to lunch with me, I'm suddenly thrown on the ground, with Nate's heavy, strong body on top of mine.

I blink once, twice, not understanding what's happened at all.

He's warm and heavy, his hips pressed against mine in the most delicious and carnal way. Our faces are just inches away and I can see the beautiful flecks of gold and green in his brown eyes. And he smells so good.

"What the..." I manage to get out.

"There was a bike," Nate explains, quickly getting up from me. I find I miss his weight on me. He points, and I see a guy on a bike still pedaling away from us. Nate picks up his jacket from the ground. "It was coming right at you..."

He gives me a hand and I pick myself up. I'm glad he doesn't let go of me. He's warm and strong, while I'm suddenly shaking like a leaf. People passing by us stare curiously. A few people ask if we're okay, and we nod. The guy on the bike is pedaling away like his life depends on it, already turning the corner.

"That was intense," I tell Nate, still holding onto his hand. "I guess you kind of... just saved my life. Or at least saved me from a broken bone or two. Thank you."

"Not a problem," he replies. His eyes flash angrily after the biker, his jawline going hard. "Damn biker. Probably a clueless kid."

"Hey." I squeeze his hand. Nate looks at me with a

worried look, and I smile to calm him down. "It's really not a big deal. I'm fine."

"Your jacket's ripped," Nate mutters. He looks me up and down, as if inspecting me for injuries that I'm not telling him about. There's a possessiveness to it that makes my stomach flutter in the best kind of way.

I pull off my jacket and there's a huge rip going down the back of it. It's pretty much unsalvageable at this point, but better it than my skin. Thankfully, it was an old sale bin bargain jacket, so I don't care about it too much.

"I'll pay that price," I say with a smile, shedding my jacket and dumping it in a nearby trash can. "You alright, by the way?"

"Yeah, I'm fine," Nate says, his smile finally returning. He still looks at me with those dangerous, possessive eyes that make me think he's going to throw me over his shoulder and take me someplace safer.

I come to stand beside him and nudge him in the ribs. "Thanks again, Nate."

He shrugs like it was nothing, and I quickly come to the understanding he doesn't want me to make a big deal out of this. Instead of pressing him, I continue walking in the direction of the sushi place. It's off the main path of "old town" but that means that it won't be quite so busy.

Nate follows behind. The tension between us is almost electric at this point, and I want to touch him badly. Not just touch him, but feel him, his heart against mine, the heat of his skin. I want his weight on me again. To be surrounded by his scent and warmth.

Get a grip, Ada, I tell myself. *He's still your boss. He's still older than you.*

But I can't help myself. Ever since Layla told me Nate

was available, I've been unable to resist temptation. And I know I'm being a fool... But I'm so glad I asked him out to lunch.

"So, have you lived here long?" I ask as we walk down the sidewalks. The sidewalks are full of students and their parents all exploring the old town area. I'm actually glad for the crowd. It gives me a good excuse to stay close to Nate and our arms keep bumping into one another as we walk.

He nods. "My parents moved us here when I was a kid. My dad was a professor. He taught mathematics." Pride and sadness tangle in his voice.

"Does he still teach?" I ask, carefully sidestepping a new freshman promising her mom that she will never visit the bar they are walking in front of.

Nate shakes his head, his eyes focusing far off down the street. "No."

I decide to change the subject. "So, what got you into coffee?"

The spark inside of him returns and he faces me with a fresh grin. "I've loved coffee forever."

"And?"

"In high school, my parents drank terrible coffee. The cheapest pre-ground stuff the grocery store could barely legally call coffee," he replies. His eyes sparkle and I can feel myself falling just a little more in love with him. "And I loved the stuff. Couldn't get enough."

I laugh. "That's not exactly what you sell at Perk Me Up."

"No, thank god," he says with a chuckle. "I have matured with my tastes, but it's what got me started. In college, I actually did some traveling. I went to South America and had actual, fresh coffee. Have you ever had real Guatemalan coffee?"

I shake my head no. "I had some really good Kona blend in Hawaii, but never Guatemalan."

He nods. "It changed how I drank coffee. I became obsessed with finding the best blends. I wanted the freshest stuff, but you have to buy it in bulk." He shrugs and chuckles as we stop at a crosswalk and wait for the light to change. "And that was the beginning of the end. I opened up a coffee shop so I could always have the best coffee."

"So you opened up a coffee shop so you could have coffee that's only sold in bulk?" I giggle and he grins at me.

A slight breeze ruffles his dark hair. The sun is high, but casting no shadows and the buildings are reflecting the light well. A storm is coming and dark clouds hover over the horizon just behind him. With his sleeves rolled up, jacket slung over his shoulder, and smile, it is a perfect picture of him. Without thinking, I pull out my camera and snap a shot of him looking thoughtfully back toward his shop. His eyes are soft and his mouth is smiling.

"Did you just take my picture?" he asks, looking at me strangely.

"Yeah... sorry." I quickly put my camera back in the bag. "It's a bad habit, but you were perfect."

"Perfect?" He raises an eyebrow. "Are you going to at least let me see it?"

"If you want."

"I want."

The way he says it, the way his eyes flicker up and down my body, makes me think he wants more than just the picture.

da

Even though it's a low budget place, I guarantee Sushi Mania has the best sushi in town. There's a trendier place where everyone takes their parents when they come to visit, but this is better. It's fresh, authentic and absolutely delicious, even if it's hidden away down a small side street.

Nate doesn't doubt me, and I order for us both after he asks me to recommend something. I love that he lets me choose. It shows he has some respect for me. And I've dated enough assholes to know that this is rare- being considered equal.

"So, do I get to see that picture?" he asks as we take a seat in a small booth near the back of the restaurant.

I pull out my camera and turn on the preview screen.

The photo is grainy in the small preview, but I know it's

good. It will look amazing in black and white, and it really brings out something about Nate. It shows his warmth and smile. He looks friendly and happy, as if he's survived the storm clouds behind him. As if they'd passed him already.

"Not bad," Nate says, peering at the image. I can tell he doesn't really think it's anything amazing, but he smiles and hands the camera back to me. "Don't I have to sign a modeling waiver or something?"

"Is it okay that I took your picture?" I ask, suddenly nervous. "I like taking them when people aren't expecting it. As soon as people see a camera, fake smiles come out, and that's the last thing I want in my photos. I want to capture people as I see them."

He looks down at the camera in my hands. "And that's how you see me?"

Smiling and handsome as hell? I think. "Yes," I say instead.

"Then you have my permission to take my photo whenever you want," he tells me. Then he pauses. "As long as they are appropriate and something I can show the café staff."

The idea that I might ever even have the opportunity to take nude or indecent photos of him has me blushing and heating. Oh, the ideas now floating around in my head.

"If I did take an indecent photo of you, I promise to only share it with you," I reply with a naughty smile of my own.

The grin he gives me has my knees spreading.

"Here's your food," the waitress announces, setting food on our table. I usually like her, she's definitely one of my favorite waitresses here, but today I wish she could have had better timing.

"So, tell me about yourself," Nate says, pouring some soy sauce into a small bowl. "Who were all those people you came in with yesterday?"

"Oh, they're my study group," I reply. "It's usually the three of us, but there's a couple of people like Amanda that join when they need to study. Amanda was the girl in the blue shirt today."

"She ordered a hot chocolate," he says, nodding.

I smile. Of course he would notice their coffee orders and not what they were wearing.

"And?" He raises an eyebrow at me, so I continue.

"There's Jacob," I continue. "He's taking photography as a minor, so we have a few classes together. He ordered the mocha latte with extra whip."

Nate slows in his chewing, swallowing slowly. "And you two study together?"

I wonder if it's jealousy I hear in his voice and if it's a good thing that I like hearing it there.

"He's a good guy, and not bad looking... I just never felt a spark, and neither did he," I explain. "He's more like a brother than anything."

"A spark is definitely important," Nate winks at me.

My heart skips a beat for the next moment, and I feel his leg brushing up against mine under the table. I nearly choke on my edamame, but manage to conceal it with a cough.

"Well err, yeah," I continue as if nothing happened.

Nate's leg returns to its rightful place beneath the table, and I keep talking.

"Jacob's studying music as his major," I explain. "He wants to play in the orchestra."

"What's his instrument?" Nate asks.

"Violin."

"Ah. I'd love to hear him play some day."

And just like that, he makes my heart skip a beat again. The fact that he's taking an interest in my friends makes me happy. Makes me smile. There's such a goodness in him that I'm seriously falling for.

"Then there's Audrey," I continue. "She's my best friend even though she's studying animal sciences. She's a vet-tech on the weekends at a local clinic, but she ends up being my usual model."

"So your friends get random pictures of them taken too?" he asks, taking a bite of his sushi.

I pull out my camera and snap his picture without even looking in the viewfinder. "Yup."

Nate just grins. "Audrey is the one with the pixie cut? That ordered an Americano?"

"Yeah," I smile."That's the one."

"She is stunning," Nate agrees.

I smile back, picking up an avocado maki with my chopsticks. I try to ignore the surge of jealousy that fires through me. Audrey *is* stunning, but I don't like hearing Nate say it. I push the avocado maki around on my plate in annoyance instead of eating it.

"Can I try that?" Nate asks, pointing to one of the avocado rolls on my plate.

"Sure." I think of just passing him the plate, but change my mind. I pick up the sushi roll with my chopsticks and zoom it into his mouth like he's a small child.

He grins at me, licking his bottom lip. Something deep in my core ignites watching his tongue flick out.

"Like avocado, do you?" I ask, watching his mouth with a hunger that has nothing to do with food.

"No, I usually don't," he admits, making a face. "I was just hoping you'd do that."

I snort in surprise and Nate winks at me.

I can't get enough of this man. He's handsome. Funny. Quirky. And not to mention handsome as hell... I want a taste.

He's older than you. He's your boss. The words repeat in my head like a mantra. I know I should listen to it, but I don't want to.

I like him.

We finish our lunch as I keep telling him about my friends and school. Nate is a great listener, but he doesn't say much about himself. I ask, but he always brings it back to me. I wish he'd open up to me a little as well. Oh well, always time for that later on. The day is young, and we'll be seeing plenty more of each other at work.

Once we're done and the waitress brings us the receipt, I reach for my wallet, but Nate stops me.

"Let me get it," he says confidently.

"No, it's fine," I reply. "I have a good job."

"Really." He grins at me. "I want to, Ada. As a thank you for showing me this place. I have a feeling I'm gonna be a regular. I can't believe I didn't know about it before."

I nod, agreeing to his terms, but thinking of something as I do.

"Alright, but only if you promise to invite me with you next time you come," I say. "You still haven't tried their mochi. A travesty, I might add."

Nate hands his card to the waitress and winks at me. "It's a deal, Newbie."

After our lunch, Nate offers to walk me home.

At first, I'm a little embarrassed about showing him where I live. I mean, I'm sure his home is amazing, having a place as successful as Perk Me Up is. My little bedroom is hardly the place to show off to anyone.

But on the other hand, I want to spend more time with him. Badly so... And I find myself agreeing to his request. We walk in the direction of my place, taking our time and talking.

The storm clouds have rolled in and the temperature has dropped. It will rain soon. The afternoon thunderstorms have started, marking the end of summer and the start of fall. It won't be long before the leaves change color and winter comes rushing in.

Despite the prior warmth of the day, I can feel autumn's cool breezes dancing across the streets.

We chat again on our way back, this time talking about our taste in movies. I'm happy to find out the man appreciates a good film, and we bond over our opinions on some 90s classics.

Despite our age differences, we have the same taste in movies. I don't feel like we're so different.

It gets chilly and windy, and I shiver and rub my arms. Nate notices.

"You cold?" he asks me.

"Kind of," I admit.

He shrugs off his blazer and offers it to me and I stare

at him for a moment too long. His sleeves are still rolled up, showing his arms. There's no tattoos, just bare muscled skin that makes me want to touch him. I wonder if he has tattoos I can't see.

"What?" Nate laughs.

"Nothing," I smile back, taking his blazer and draping it over my shoulders. "You're just a gentleman, is all. Rare to find one of those these days, it seems."

He smiles and we continue walking towards my place. I let the scent of Nathaniel Rhodes envelop me, all pine needles and coffee. Masculine and incredibly tempting.

"This is me," I finally say when we reach my door. "I'll be fine getting up by myself..."

"Are you trying to get rid of me?" Nate asks with a cocked eyebrow, and before I get a chance to respond, he invades my personal space by stepping closer, pressing me against the front door. His arm presses into the door above me, the other caging me in.

I could get out if I wanted to. He's left me an easy escape, but I wouldn't leave if you paid me.

"I..." I start to say, but I'm interrupted when my boss places a finger on my lips.

"Ada..." he says roughly. "I just want to thank you for inviting me to lunch. I needed that break badly."

"Not a problem," I manage to choke out.

My heart is threatening to jump straight out of my chest, and I'm so terribly desperate for him to do something - touch me, kiss me, talk some more... Anything, just so I can get another dose of Nathaniel Rhodes.

"I hope we'll do it again soon," I add.

"Me too," Nate admits. "Ada... I want to kiss you."

Again, that skipping-a-beat thing. My palms are

sweating. I'm getting butterflies. And I still haven't answered him.

"Yes... Please," I breathe.

Nate's lips are on mine as soon as the words leave my lips. I'm so damn desperate to taste him I melt against his mouth as soon as it touches mine.

I moan softly against his lips and he grabs me by the hips, pulling me closer.

Nate kisses nothing like I imagined he would. There is none of the gentleness, kindness or attention he showed me throughout lunch.

Instead, his kiss is possessive, almost rough, demanding yet sensual.

And I love it.

We break apart moments later, and I still taste him on my lips. He's full-blown masculinity, like something out of a perfume ad. And under the musk and woody scents, there is the unmistakable aroma of coffee. The taste, the scent, the essence of Perk Me Up. All on this man's lips.

It makes me smile like a fool.

"I'll see you at work tomorrow," Nate tells me with a grin.

"Yeah..." I reply breathlessly.

He winks at me and walks off. It is only a moment later that I realize he doesn't even have my number, and my fingers are already itching to text him a thank you for the lovely day we spent together.

"Nate!" I call out after him.

He turns to face me, and I blush.

"I, uh... Don't you want my number?" I ask awkwardly.

Nate laughs.

"Don't need it, Newbie. It's all over your paperwork. Remember who I am?" he grins at me.

"My boss?" I reply, his smile mirrored on my face.

"Exactly," Nathaniel replies. "I got you right where I want you. Right under me. Bye, Newbie."

He walks off, leaving me blushing like a madman. I'm still wearing his blazer, and I don't want to call out after him a second time, so I let it sit snugly against my shoulders.

And if I was questioning Nate's lack of interest only a moment ago, all of that is temporarily forgotten as I'm left smitten with the new man in my life.

ate

I haven't loved coming into work this much since I first opened.

All this week, Ada has been on the morning shift for training. Not that she needs it. The girl picked up the coffees and how to make them like a pro. The espresso machine hums under her fingers and she makes a better latte than Sydney.

I wish I could say it was my training, but it is definitely Layla's influence.

I've also eaten lunch the last three days, which definitely helps my mood. I often forget to eat when I'm working. Half my meals are random muffins I find in the kitchen or sandwiches that Layla slides onto my desk when I'm not looking.

But not today. This week, I'm eating lunch with Ada.

I didn't mean for it to happen, but I can't keep myself away from her. The day after sushi, I invited her to try my favorite restaurant. It's a burrito shop that sells breakfast burritos all day.

She'd loved it.

I loved that she'd told me how she got into photography.

"My dad had this old camera from college," she said, chewing happily on her burrito. "I found it when I was ten. My mom hated that I took pictures of everything, but my dad was so proud. He'd print them out and hang them up all over the house."

She'd then proceeded to tell me all about photography. She described lenses and apertures, lighting and shutter speed. She said she liked digital photos better than the film, which she said probably made her a terrible photographer.

I'd walked her home and kissed her again. Even though I wanted to pick her up, carry her into her bed and show her the most pleasure of her life, I was trying my best to go slow. She was still my employee.

So I settled for just a kiss that made my body ache for a release I couldn't have.

The next day, she'd suggested the sandwich shop next door.

I'd never been so excited to eat a sub in all my life.

Lunchtime comes and I'm practically dancing like a puppy about to go on a walk. I'm pacing the space of my desk, counting down the minutes until her shift is over and we can leave.

I am seriously considering giving her more "training" shifts just so we can keep having lunch. Once she switches to her real shifts in the afternoon and evenings, these lunch dates won't be so easy to arrange.

She knocks on my office door and grins when she sees me.

"You ready?" Her voice is sweet and bright.

I've been ready for hours, but I just nod and we head out of the shop. Sydney is still staring at us like we have six heads, but I don't care.

"How about this place?" she asks, motioning to the sandwich shop next door. "Have you eaten here before?"

It's less than ten steps from my coffee shop, so I nod. I'm not that much of a workaholic. I do get out occasionally.

"The owner and I trade lunches and coffee," I explain. Some weeks, I'm fairly certain that these sandwiches are the only thing I've eaten. That and day old pastries in the shop. I tend to focus too much on my work and forget to eat.

"I haven't tried it yet," she says as we walk in. "What's good?"

I desperately try to think of the best thing on the menu, but all I can think about is how pretty her hair is in the sunlight. She's wearing a simple pale blue t-shirt that skims her curves but doesn't show them off. It looks good against the warmth of her skin.

"Everything," I answer, but really I mean everything about her.

I know I should slow down. I know that I'm falling for her way too fast.

She's my employee. She's younger than me.

I'm falling into my old bad habits: see a girl, fall in love too fast, pull away because I'm terrified of actual love, realize that I'm a terrible person, girl moves on, heartbreak.

But Ada is a balm to my soul. When she's around, I smile. I laugh.

I feel like I haven't laughed in years.

And I don't want to give that up.

She orders a turkey on wheat, all the veggies, and ranch on the side.

I order something. It doesn't even matter what. We go to the table next to the window and I barely taste my food. It could have been sawdust or heaven's ambrosia and I wouldn't have cared.

Ada is smiling and I can't help but smile too.

"Class starts soon, right?" I ask, taking a bite of my sandwich. It might be ham?

"On Monday." She quickly swallows. "Actually, I'm pretty excited about a couple of them. One is actually going to have a videography component. I haven't done video work, but I think it will be interesting. I'm also taking a course on social media and marketing that is going to be super interesting."

I pause while chewing. "They have a class on social media?"

I feel old. A college course on social media. I had classes on how to use a computer, but kids these days seem to be born knowing how to use the internet.

"Yeah!" Ada lights up. "It's going to cover all the major players and how to adjust views and marketing techniques. There is a lot of how to figure out the algorithms since they change so often and how to change marketing to suit."

Algorithms? Marketing?

I feel older still.

"How interesting," I say. "I have to say, I don't know much about marketing. Just a few Facebook ads here and there."

"You're still on Facebook?" She sounds scandalized. "That's for old people."

Suddenly, I feel every gray hair on my head. I feel every wrinkle, every sore body part, every aching bone. I look at this youthful, energetic young woman, and I feel ancient.

She sets her sandwich down. "Actually, I wanted to talk to you about something."

I swallow hard. The bread of my sandwich scratches my throat the whole way down. This is where she tells me that I'm too old for her. That this is going to work.

I don't blame her. It's only ten years or so, but right now, it feels like a lifetime. She doesn't even know all the baggage that comes with me.

She fiddles with the silver bird charm on her necklace.

"Would it be okay if I did some social media marketing for the café?"

I blink twice. That wasn't what I was expecting. "What?"

"Just some posts and videos for various social media sites. I noticed you don't have accounts on several platforms, which is a real missed opportunity," she says, her words coming out fast. "I just want to do some basic stuff. No ads or money needed. Just posts. Some videos, but everything will be marketable."

"Um, sure?"

She grins. "Thank you. It'll really help me out for my class."

"Happy to help," I reply. I'm not quite sure what I've just agreed to.

"You have no idea what I'm talking about, do you?" she asks, setting her sandwich down. She's smiling, a glint in her eye that has me wary.

I could lie, but I think she would see through it faster than a tech bubble crash.

She just chuckles. "I plan on making some videos about our coffee. Sydney has already agreed to be my actress. We'll do them as they come in as orders, so we won't even be wasting coffee."

I nod, but I have no idea what she's talking about. I do like that she called it "our" coffee.

"Then, I'll post them on TikTok and some other social media sites. We'll get the word out about the coffees we have."

Suddenly it clicks in my brain and I feel like I could kiss her.

"You're amazing," I tell her. If she can get more customers in, I may not have to depend on that stupid caramel coffee to save everything.

She smiles at me and my whole world lights up.

"How does this help you with your classes?" I ask.

"We're supposed to do this promo stuff for ourselves, but I don't want to focus on me," she explains. "I have a lot more ideas for the coffee shop. And I don't need to market myself. I'd rather market my favorite place."

She blushes slightly and looks quickly down at the table.

God, I want to kiss her so bad.

So I do.

I ignore the fact that we are in public. That we're right

next door to my store. That she is my employee and my junior.

She kisses me back, sweet and tender, before pulling away and blushing. No one in the store is looking at us, but she glances around like they are all staring.

But she grins at me and I feel like I'm on top of the world.

ate

"Good morning, Nate," Sydney greets me Friday morning. She's waiting by the front door for me to open the shop. It's still dark outside, but the morning rush waits for no man.

"Good morning, Sydney," I reply. She grins. I've given her permission to call me Nate. It felt like I should. She and Ada were now best buddies, and since I was dating Ada, it didn't feel right. At least, it felt like I was dating Ada. Nothing was official yet.

"There was a note for you on the door," Sydney says, handing me an envelope.

I thank her and take the envelope. She starts opening up the shop, turning on lights and starting pots of coffee to brew. Ada should be in any minute, and I glance out the big front windows looking for her bright smile.

She's not here yet, so I take the letter to my office. The front is addressed to me, but there is no return address. My stomach does a twist that makes me glad I haven't eaten yet.

It's another invoice for my loan. I didn't take this loan out from a traditional bank, so the notices are not traditional.

Payment due.

That's all it says, but it makes my blood run cold and my skin go clammy.

I close the door to my office and start pulling up every financial ledger I can find. If I'm creative, I can make this payment. It's been a decent month at the coffee shop. I'm sure I can find the loan money due if I look hard enough.I can feel the weight of the loan on my shoulders like a mountain. A mountain that is going to destroy my business. My employees will lose their jobs, jobs that many of them depend on for survival. And not just my employees. I can't let this destroy them all.

My mood sours. I'm irritated and annoyed, and no one knows it better than I do. I steer clear of Ada for the whole of Friday. I don't want to bring her down. I don't want to ruin this beautiful golden sunshine between us with my gray sourness.

I know she stopped at my office for lunch, but I kept the door closed. I don't want to taint her life with my mistakes. Besides, I need to find the funds to pay this month's payment.

Saturday comes, and I bury myself in accounting and payroll. I hide in my office, doing the mind-numbing work to keep my brain from thinking. I think I found a solution to this month's payment. It's not a great solution, but it means I have another month to come up with a better one.

If I don't pay myself and I wait another week to make an inventory purchase, I can make it. It's not a solution I can do again. I don't mind not paying myself, but without inventory, I can't make money. We can squeak by on what we have this week.

I spend the entire day holed up in my office, trying to think of another solution to the money problem. Coming up empty-handed, my stomach rumbling, and my brain craving caffeine, I finally decide to grab a cup of coffee. I haven't made any real progress on my caramel coffee either. It's just one more thing that's making me feel a little pissed off.

It's late evening when I emerge from my office and walk through the kitchen, picking up and stuffing my face with a leftover blueberry scone. I inhale it so quickly I don't even taste it. I can't remember the last meal I ate. Probably the one with Ada. Something aches where my heart should be.

I step out into the main area behind the counter, only to find Ada. I remember that today is her first day off of training, and thus she's on the afternoon-to-closing shift. She smiles at me with some hesitation. I feel like shit, and also guilty as fuck for neglecting her yesterday.

Thunder rumbles outside. It's already dark out, but a storm is rolling in as they often do in the evenings. I really did work the entire day away. I look at my watch and see that it's nearly closing time.

"Hey, Newbie," I greet Ada as she's cleaning up the counter.

"Hi."

I can't tell anything from her tone. She doesn't move away from me or glare at me, but she doesn't use my name either.

"So, how'd the afternoon shift go?" I ask.

She shrugs. "It was easy after yesterday. Layla showed me how to do everything. It's just the morning stuff in reverse."

I nod, picking up one of the cleaning cloths and starting to wipe down the cabinets under the espresso machines.

She's already done most of the work of emptying the coffee pots, cleaning the espresso machines, and all the restocking for tomorrow. I glance at some of the items and cringe.

That late inventory purchase is going to be super close.

"Did I do something wrong?" she asks, stopping and looking at me.

"What? No." I look around at the counters and shop. She's done a great job closing up, so I shake my head. "It looks like you closed up everything perfectly."

Her mouth thins. "That's not what I meant." She takes a deep breath, as if trying to steady herself. "I mean, with us."

Guilt and that pang in my chest comes back. "What do you mean?"

"Yesterday..." She chews on her bottom lip in a way that makes me want to kiss it. "I thought we'd have lunch, but... you stayed in your office. And I still don't have your phone number."

She looks at me with big eyes. She thought it was her

fault I hid in my office all day. And I didn't call her, so she had no way to get a hold of me.

I'm an idiot.

"I know we're kind of going slow, but I thought that was okay. I mean, I don't mind going slow. Or fast, or... I don't know. I just thought you were mad at me or that you didn't want to see me anymore or that you didn't want to date an employee. If we are dating? I don't know what we're doing, but I thought–"

I cross the small space behind the register and kiss her before she can say another word. At first she stiffens, but then melts into me. Her body feels so good in mine, pressed together in all the right places. I love the feel of her hands on my back, holding onto me.

"You did nothing wrong," I assure her. I brush a strand of hair from her forehead. "I just got wrapped up in business stuff. I swear it had nothing to do with us."

"Oh." Her lips make a beautiful shape and her cheeks are flushed. She smiles up at me. "So we're okay?"

I curse myself. I should have at least said hello yesterday. I didn't need to be such a grump that I couldn't at least have some semblance of manners.

"Very okay." I kiss her again. I intend for the kiss to be short and sweet, but she tastes so good that the kiss lingers. Her lips, her tongue, her mouth all taste like coffee and sweetness.

I can't get enough. I could taste her all day and never be satisfied.

She pulls away, still flushed.

"We should finish up," she says, not moving away from me.

"Yeah. We should." For a moment, I consider just

pushing her up against the cabinets and showing her how wild she drives me.

But she's done such a nice job of cleaning them that I'd hate to ruin her effort. Plus, there are very large windows looking out over the street and still a few people outside walking to bars.

She smiles at me, and for the first time all day, I feel better. The constant weight of the world on my shoulders suddenly doesn't feel quite so crushing. It's still there, but it's no longer going to kill me.

I help her finish cleaning everything, wiping down tables and chairs and sweeping the floor. The work goes quickly and we have it done in minutes.

"Can I walk you home?" I ask. I'm not really worried about her. It's a small town and it's not far, but I still worry. Plus, her smile is the only thing that made my day better and I'm not ready to give it up just yet.

"Sure." She grins at me, shouldering her backpack. It looks full and heavy but she declines my offer to carry it.

We head out the front door, and just as I turn the key in the lock, thunder rumbles hard enough to shake the glass.

"We should probably hurry," Ada says, glancing up at the dark sky.

I nod, and we quickly hurry out to the street. We only make it one block before the heavens open up. It's not a little rain, but a deluge.

Ada reaches into her bag and pulls out my jacket, covering the two of us. I guess she hasn't had the chance to return it just yet. I have been steering clear of her for the past two days, which would make it hard.

"Huh, this looks familiar," I tease, motioning to the jacket. She grins at me.

We laugh as the rain hits us and find a less drippy place in the side alley between a bar and a Tex-mex restaurant. There's a small awning, just big enough for the two of us to hide under. It quickly becomes apparent the rain won't stop, as it's coming down hard. I'm just about to suggest for us to head back to the shop, when I hear a small whimpering sound.

"Do you hear that?" I ask Ada over the sound of the rain.

"Yeah," she responds with her eyebrows knitted together in worry.

"Almost sounds like a..."

Realization hits us both at the same time, and we leave the safe haven we've sought refuge in, and start digging through the trash piled next to the dumpsters.

There's piles of boxes, rotting food, empty beer bottles, and things I really don't want to wade through. But now I'm determined. I want to find the source of that whimpering.

"Here," Ada calls out to me, pointing frantically to the largest dumpster. "Right here."

I approach her and realize she is right - the whimpers are coming from the bottom of the dumpster. But there's no way we can reach in there - it's too deep down.

I look down at my pants and silently wish them a fond farewell.

"I'm going in," I announce, rolling up my shirtsleeves. I debate if I should take my shoes off. I don't want to ruin them, but there is a high likelihood of broken glass.

The creature in the dumpster whimpers again, a sad

frightened sound that makes Ada's eyes dart to the dumpster.

I sigh. I'll buy new shoes.

I climb into the dumpster, trying not to think about all the things a Tex-Mex restaurant and bar might throw away.

I don't care about any of that. I just hope we're not too late...

CHAPTER 10

*N*ate

Things squish beneath my feet that I don't want to think about. The smell makes me gag, but I'm glad there are only a few trash bags in the dumpster. The whining is louder now, as if the thing stuck in here knows someone is looking for it.

Moments later, I emerge with a box in my hands. I hand the box over to Ada and climb down to safety.

She carries the box over to the shelter of the awning with me not far behind. The box is taped shut, but Ada has it ripped open before I can even reach for my pocket knife.

A pair of chocolate brown, sad eyes look back at me.

"Oh, you poor thing," Ada coos, picking up the small puppy and cuddling it to her cheek. It's small, light colored, and fluffy. A tiny pink tongue darts out and licks her cheek. She looks at me with big eyes.

"Let's go back to Perk Me Up," I tell her. She wraps my jacket around the puppy. We leave the box in the alley since it's soaked with dumpster water.

We sprint through the rainy streets, and luckily there's no one out in this weather. I have the door open in seconds and we burst inside, breathing hard.

I lock up behind us and we take a moment to catch our breaths as it starts to pour down even more on the other side of the door.

We're both soaked through and through, both shivering.

Ada puts the jacket down on a table, and if on cue, a small head peeks out from the fabric.

"Who the hell puts a puppy in a dumpster?" I ask, not really wanting an answer.

We both stare in wonder at the small, sandy colored puppy who crawls out of the jacket. It's shivering as well, and looking scared and vulnerable.

Something tugs on my heartstrings, looking at the poor, defenseless little critter. I might even think it's love if I didn't know myself better. The pup is pretty adorable.

"It's a boy," Ada tells me upon closer inspection, and I can't help but reach out and pet the little guy's head. He's filthy, but adorable.

"You love him already," Ada says right away.

"Shut up," I reply with a hidden grin. "I just don't get how people can be so fucking heartless."

My second statement makes us both question the nature of the person who left the puppy out in the rain.

Worse than that, sealed in a box in a dumpster. If we hadn't found him, he wouldn't be alive come morning.

"This is freaking terrible," I say, running a hand through my soaking wet hair.

"I'll take him," Ada pipes up.

"Does your landlord let you have animals?" I ask doubtfully, and she doesn't reply, which answers my question

"I'll figure something out," she replies, a stubborn set to her jaw that I find incredibly attractive.

"First things first," I tell Ada. "Let's head up,get on some dry clothes, and get a blanket for the puppy."

Ada nods in agreement, then stops in her tracks before following me down the hallway to my office.

"What do you mean, 'up'?" she asks doubtfully. "What's in the back? I thought only your office was back there."

I hesitate before answering, but only for a moment. Might as well tell her the truth, especially if I plan on keeping her around.

"I live on the second floor," I explain. "The building belongs to my family. My apartment's on the second floor, and Perk Me Up is on the ground."

Ada's eyes widen in surprise, but I'm not in the mood to chat about my living arrangements - or, god forbid, my family - so I just motion for her to follow me into the back.

She grabs the puppy, despite the fact that it's soaking wet and stinky as hell, and follows me through the kitchen. Once we reach my office, I head to the left and open a small door leading into a stairway. It's small and the cement stairs echo with our wet footsteps.

We walk up the stairs until we arrive in the main area

of my loft. It's an enormous space, dining room, kitchen and living room all together. I've furnished it pretty modern, back when I had some money to spare and didn't give a fuck about anything or anyone besides myself.

"You want some fresh clothes?" I ask Ada.

"Yours?" she replies, blushing lightly.

She's so damn adorable.

"Yeah, mine," I grin at her.

I open a door that leads into the closet, and Ada follows me inside with wonder in her eyes. It's a big closet. Once again, I'm making an impression on her - not that I want to. Not with my closet, anyway. Once again, it is a remnant of the old me, the me who didn't give a fuck about anything that wasn't labeled with an expensive brand's name.

I grab two pairs of sweatpants, two plain black t-shirts, and two pairs of boxers from their stacks in my closet. It's not exactly the most feminine of clothes, but I figure she'd appreciate anything dry. I then quickly close the doors behind me. She gives me a weird look, and I shrug.

"Don't want the puppy dragging dirt in there," I admit. I give the dog the side-eye. "He probably just wants to eat my shoes."

Guess there's a piece of me that's still the prick I used to be way back when.

"You can take a shower if you want," I say, laying the clothes out on my bed and motioning to the bathroom. "Some hot water would probably feel better.".

She nods, but seems a little apprehensive, so I laugh out loud.

"Nervous about leaving me alone with the pup?" I ask.

Ada shifts from one foot to another uncomfortably,

thus confirming my thought. She's worked with me enough now to know that I'm a bit of a clean freak. The fact that there is puppy mud all over the floor is making my eye start to twitch.

"It'll be fine, I promise," I say to her.

And to solidify my statement, I take the puppy out of her hands. The dog wriggles, and droplets of rainwater fall from his coat, dirtying up my floor.

I grimace and hold the dog out away from me. Ada raises one eyebrow.

"Go take a shower," I tell her. "It'll be fine."

She looks skeptically at me and then the dog, but then looks wistfully at the shower like it's calling her name. I can see goosebumps all up and down her arms and she's shivering.

Finally, she sighs and heads to the shower, leaving me with the very stinky, very wet, very messy dog.

I notice she doesn't lock the door, even though she very well could, and that fills me with all kinds of excitement.

I could go in and join her. I want a shower myself. And it would feel so good to have her naked in the steamy water...

But the puppy whines and I remember that I'm now alone with a canine I have no idea what to do with. In the end, I place the pup on the floor, where he immediately proceeds to make a puddle of pee.

I sigh and roll my eyes before reaching for some paper towels and mopping everything up. Of course, by the time I'm done, Mr. Puppy has made another puddle a few feet away.

"For fuck's sake," I mutter to myself, but I can't help laughing a little.

There's no denying that the dog is pretty adorable, even though he's a messy little thing.

"You need a bath too," I tell him. I go to the big kitchen sink and start to run the warm water. All I have is dish soap, but if it's gentle enough to use on ducklings, it's probably safe to use on dirty dogs.

He whines as I put him down in the sink, his little claws scrambling against the stainless steel.

"It's okay," I coo to him. He's shivering, but he lets me give him a quick bath. I even manage to wrap him up in the dish towel before he can spray water all over everything.

"I bet you're hungry," I say to him. He cocks his head at me like he understands what I'm saying. He looks so pathetic with his curly fur all wet, But at least he's warm now and doesn't smell like rotting refried beans.

Finally, I decide some leftover mac-and-cheese will have to do, as I have absolutely nothing else in my fridge, and I don't want the dog to starve - god knows how long it's been since he last ate.

I heat up the food - no idea why, guess it's just instinct - and present it to the puppy on one of my expensive-as-fuck plates. The dog gives me an unimpressed look and I sigh.

"Look bud, that's the best I have until tomorrow morning," I explain to the puppy. "You better take it."

It almost feels as if the dog sighs before tucking into his dinner, macaroni and grated cheese flying everywhere. He sure looks to be hungry. I suddenly realize that I probably should have waited on the bath until after he'd eaten.

I set up a little bowl of water next to the dish, and the puppy laps it up, sloshing water everywhere.

I sigh and grab some more paper towels.

I feel horrible about the state we found him in, and I can't help but wish I could've caught the person who discarded him in our back alley. It's been a while since my last fist-fight, but I'm sure I can still kick some serious ass, just like the good old times.

I hear the bathroom door opening a few moments later, and I look up, unprepared for what I am about to see.

Ada's wearing my sweats and my shirt. The sweats hang low on her hips, too big for her, yet somehow showing off her amazing curves. Her hair is wet, and it makes the shirt stick to her skin. I can still see the tips of her nipples poking at the fabric and I can't help but stare.

I'm sure my eyes are about to bug out of my head and I can feel blood rushing south. She looks spectacular and I can't help the three steps I take toward her.

"I, uh," she begins, running a hand through her wet hair. "I didn't know where you kept your hair dryer."

She blushes and I grin at her. Fuck, she was adorable before, but now?

She's hot as hell, and I want my hands all over her. I want to make her mine. I want to claim those curves, kiss her lips, and see how those nipples feel in my mouth.

"I see you've made friends," Ada says with a grin as she approaches the dog.

He's just finished his impromptu-dinner and has now laid down his head on his front paws. His curly fur is drying in little ringlets and his ears are wonderfully floppy. He really is an adorable puppy. There's no denying that, and I'm not even a dog person.

"Do you mind watching him for a bit while I jump in the shower myself?" I ask Ada, pointing towards the puppy. "If you could put our stuff in the dryer, that would be awesome as well."

Ada is quick to nod and we smile at each other. I strip down my shirt, feeling her eyes on my body as I hand it to her. I probably could have waited until I was in the bathroom, but I want her eyes on me. I want her to stare at me like I'm staring at her.

"Laundry room is next to the closet, to the right," I say.

"Got it."

Ada's eyes linger cheekily on my body before coming up to meet my eyes. She plays with her necklace like she's thinking of doing something. Her eyes go up and down my body again, her tongue flicking out to lick her lips.

She takes a step toward me and her upper lip curls in disgust.

"You should shower," she says, pointing to a spot of mud on my cheek. "You smell terrible."

CHAPTER 11

da

Nate disappears into the bathroom. I reach down and pet the puppy. He wags his tail and sighs with pleasure.

He's a cute little thing. I suspect he's part poodle mixed with something. The curly fur is very poodle, but his nose isn't the right shape. Either way, he's adorable. He looks up at me and blinks slowly before settling back down.

I ball my clothes along with Nate's shirt in my hands and head for the laundry room.

Truth be told, I was being a little tease coming out here wet. I let the sweatpants hang low on my hips and I didn't hide how the cold air after the shower affected me, but I couldn't resist it - I wanted to see what Nate's reaction would be. And he did not disappoint.

The way his eyes roamed my body, lingering on my body, and the slight hiss as he breathed in too quickly made me feel hot and heavy all over. It made me want to feel his hands, his fingers on me. But he didn't make a move... and so neither did I.

All he's done is kiss me. And while they were fantastic kisses, I want more. I just thought we were going slow since we worked together. It was smart for us to go slow and make sure we weren't going to do something we would regret. It was safe. It is the smart thing, the strategic thing, which is entirely Nate's MO. But right now, I don't want to go slow. I want to speed up and go as fast as we can. I want to feel every inch of him.

It's getting late now, definitely past midnight. I should be back at home, but then again, tomorrow is Sunday and I'll be able to sleep in.My shift doesn't start until the afternoon.

A thousand thoughts race through my head as I put our wet clothes in the dryer. Nate in the shower. The way he'd heroically jumped into the garbage dumpster. The sweet way he looked at the puppy. The way he looked at me.

I stare at the dryer. It's a fancy one, and I'm struggling to understand what I'm supposed to do with it, which makes me feel dumb as hell. There's so many buttons and knobs, all with settings that make no sense to me. Really, what is the difference between cotton, casual, and wrinkle free? I want all of those things.

Finally, I set it on a program that I think will work, and head back to the main room. I hear the sound of the shower running in the bathroom and I'm tempted, so very tempted, to just walk inside and catch Nate in the middle of washing himself.

I could risk a peek... But I shouldn't.

I start moving toward the sound of water. I can just imagine the way the warm water sluices down his skin, the way it would slide down his chest and slip low against his hips...

I stop myself just in time, knowing this isn't a good idea. I shouldn't be fantasizing about him... but why not? We've been flirting back and forth this whole week, and save for the weird last two days, I thought something really might happen between the two of us.

But he's been giving me the cold shoulder all Friday, and even today until we found the puppy together. I've been wondering what came over Nate and why he's acting so differently, but I haven't come to a solution just yet.

I hear the bathroom door opening with a creak and Nate emerges, his hair wet from the shower. He's wearing matching sweatpants to mine and a T-shirt. Of course, since he's still wet, it clings close to his skin, not leaving much to the imagination.

"That felt good," he remarks, and I smile at him. He glances around the room, spying the sleeping puppy. The little guy is fast asleep on the plush carpet, his head resting demurely on his front paws.

Nate motions toward the barstools at the kitchen counter. I slide onto one while Nate goes around into the kitchen and pulls out a bottle of liquor from a cabinet. I give him a questioning look, but he merely grabs two glasses from the cabinet as well.

"We deserve a drink to warm us up," he explains as he pours us each a small amount.

We clink glasses and I down the amber liquid in one gulp, nearly choking as fiery flames envelop my stomach.

"Holy hell" I exhale, coughing and trying to catch my breath.

"Yeah, you may want to go easy on that one," Nate laughs. "It's a 12 year old Scotch. Show it some respect. It's not a shot."

I look at him, feeling like he's scolded me like a little girl, but his wide grin convinces me he's just playing around.

"A gift from my dad," Nate adds, his voice quieter now.

"That's nice," I reply as he carefully pours two fingers into the glass.

This time I drink slowly, savoring the taste of the liquor on my tongue. It does taste good - rich and decadent. It reminds me of Nate.

"Are you two close?" I try to keep up the conversation about his father, since he hasn't mentioned any family at all up to this point.

I'm kind of desperate for Nate to open up to me a little, but so far it seems like he's closed off like a shell. Get too close and he'll clam up again, denying access to the private corners of his mind. I want to know him, know how he thinks. I find him fascinating and I just wish he'd open up to me.

But apparently tonight is not that night.

"Not anymore," he says simply, downing his drink in one go even though he just scolded me for doing the very same thing.

He gets up from his stool before I can comment, and walks over to the dog. He crosses his arm, but his eyes soften as he watches the puppy's back feet twitch in a dream.

I join him as he stares at the puppy, standing close

enough that we could touch, but far enough to give him the space he so obviously needs.

"You know I meant it," I tell him in a soft voice so as not to wake the dog up. "I'd be happy to take him. I'll find a way to deal with my landlord."

"I..." Nate starts. He seems a little thrown off as he looks at me. "I'd like to keep him."

I'm surprised, and as hard as I try not to show it, I'm always like an open book, and Nate reads me just with one look at my face.

"I've never had a dog, but..." He looks back at the puppy and smiles gently. "I'd really like to keep him.

I actually think it's kind of sweet how the little pup has already found a way into Nate's heart. I'd noticed the macaroni and cheese, the bath, and the bowl of water. I'd noticed how Nate's eyes soften and the age falls off of him.

I smile a little. The dog has gotten into his heart, the way that only dogs can. If anyone needs some warmth and unconditional love, I think Nate does.

"I think that's a great idea," I tell him.

Nate gets a blanket from the couch after giving me a thankful smile, and wraps the pup in it. The dog doesn't stir once, caught up in a dream. He lets out the cutest puppy sigh of contentment once he's safely enclosed in the warmth of the woolen blanket.

He goes to the fireplace and flicks a switch. A bright fire springs up in the hearth, full of dancing flames.

"I know it's a little early in the season for a fire, but with the rain, I thought it would be nice," Nate explains. He gives me a bashful smile that makes him look young and innocent.

He sits on the expensive-looking gray couch facing the fire and looks at me to join him. I move slowly, sitting close, but not too close. I'm still not sure what we're doing.

Kisses are cheap. They don't mean love.

I'm feeling a little bit awkward. Vulnerable, because I'm not in my own home, and shy, because it feels oddly intimate to be wearing Nate's clothes. It does feel nice though, and I really appreciate the offer.

He drapes a soft blanket around the both of us. It's oddly sweet and intimate, and my heart speeds up a little. I'm suddenly feeling much warmer and it has nothing to do with the blanket. We both watch the fire dance and shimmer for a moment.

"Hey," he says softly.

"Hey," I reply.

His eyes are so beautiful, especially in the firelight. There is a warm gold tone in them that sparkles, but hints of a fertile green hiding in the warm browns. I feel the beat of my heart picking up. I want him to touch me. Even just extend his hand and put it on my knee. I'd kill for that right now.

And it seems like Nate is reading my mind, as he leans forward and gently places an arm on the back of the couch behind my neck. I take a sharp intake of breath, as his warm skin touches the back of my neck.

His touch is everything I want.

"Kiss me," he whispers, curling his fingers into my damp hair and bringing me to his lips.

I'm nervous as hell. I want him so badly I'm practically shaking. The few kisses we've shared keep sneaking into my thoughts, hinting at so much more. If his kisses make my heart race and toes curl, what would it be like to have more?

But now, with Nate's lips only inches away from mine, I can barely contain myself. I need to touch him. Kiss him. Taste him. Have him for myself.

I lean forward ever so slowly, until my lips and gently on Nate's. His mouth is cold from the weather outside, his lips cool as I part them with my tongue. He groans under my probing mouth, opening wide for me. And it's all I need to let go completely.

I kiss him gently, unlike him the last time we played this game. Where Nate is demanding, I am patient. He is selfish, I offer myself to him completely. He's strong and I am weak at the knees for him.

He takes my face in his hands and pulls me closer harshly, and I rest a hand on his lap. My mind is spinning, and I know I won't be able to hold back much longer.

I need him inside me. Touching me. Fucking me, hard.

There is a strange noise coming from somewhere in the house. I ignore it, desperate for his kisses, needing his touch. I want him so badly I'm shaking.

The noise grows louder until it's no longer something we can ignore. Nate pulls back, his hands still tangled in my hair.

"What on earth is that?" Nate asks me with a furrowed brow.

I shrug, having no idea what could be making a sound like that.

Then, a loud sound tears through the apartment, shattering the moment for us.

Nate's on his feet in an instant, looking for the source of the racket.

We both look in the direction of the pup, but the dog is still safe and sound, wrapped in his blankie. Then I realize the noise is coming from the laundry room, and gulp down my fears - or at least attempt to.

"I think... I may have messed up something in the laundry room," I admit to Nate.

Right away, he heads into the other room, and I follow him rather sheepishly. I feel nervous as hell as breaking his dryer is the last thing I need right now, when I'm trying to sleep with the man.

As soon as we walk in the laundry room, the sound is very clearly coming from the dryer. The machine is rattling so much it nearly jumps off the floor, and with a groan, Nate pulls the plug from the electric socket.

It finally stills, but sparks are flying from the plug now, and I cover my face with my hands. Holy hell, what a story for my friends. Way to go, Ada.

"I'm so sorry," I rush to get the words out. "It felt like something was off when I was putting the clothes in."

I'm rushing to get through the explanation as Nate approaches me with a stern face. I feel like he's about to yell at me like I'm a child, but when my word vomit finally dies down, he merely grins at me and drops the plug.

"Don't worry about it, Ada," he tells me with a smile. "The machine's temperamental. The electricity in this building is so weird, it sometimes makes it spark. It's an old building, so it has some strange quirks."

"Oh," I reply stupidly. "So I didn't break it?"

"It isn't your fault. It does this from time to time," he tells me.

I can't believe he'd tease me like that, but I can't help but smile.

"The bad news is," Nate begins, "your clothes are almost surely fried now."

"Fried?" I repeat.

"Fried. Finito," Nate shrugs. "It's the electricity. It either goes out or comes in and messes with the dryer. I barely use it anymore."

"Okay," I add, nodding. "Do you mind if I borrow your clothes, then? I can bring them back to work tomorrow. I just need them to get home..."

"Yes," Nate interrupts my monologue. "I actually do mind."

"Oh," I fidget nervously with my necklace.

He reaches me in a few steps, and puts his hand on my fingers, stopping me from sliding the bird charm up and down the chain.

I look up at him slowly, his eyes dark and passionate, boring into mine.

"I want you to take them off," Nate tells me softly.

I open my mouth to speak, but no words come out. I'm frozen to the spot. Thankfully, Nate doesn't seem to be having the same problem.

Nate tugs at the sweatpants, easily pulling them over my hips. I kick the pants to the side, where they slide along the tile floor. His eyes take in my bare legs up to the boxers he's loaned me and the thin t-shirt. I can see my nipples practically poking holes through the fabric.

Nate licks his lips and reaches for the waistband of the boxers. His hands are warm on my bare skin, but his touch still elicits goosebumps. He wears a cocky grin as he tugs the boxers down over my hips and lets them fall to the floor.

The shirt is long enough that it covers me. Barely. I swallow hard and look up at him. His pupils are wide with desire and he's looking at me like I'm a steak and he's very hungry. I shiver, feeling vulnerable and scared as fuck. But one thing is for sure.

I want this.

So very badly.

Slowly, he reaches out toward the hem of my shirt. He pauses, giving me the opportunity to step away.

But I step closer to him. HIs fingers caress the curve of my hip as he lifts the shirt up and over my head. He takes a sharp breath as the fabric clears my breasts. I can't see him with the shirt in the way, but I can feel his body stiffen.

He tosses the shirt to the side with the sweats and stares at me in a way that makes me feel like a model. I want to flaunt my body and hide at the same time.

There's a special kind of vulnerability in being naked next to him completely clothed... And I think I like it.

"Nate..." My voice comes out breathy. "Take your clothes off."

"No," he shakes his head with that signature smirk.

With a swift move, he turns me around until my palms are braced on the walls of the room. He stands behind me, putting a free hand on the small of my back. I arch involuntarily for him, needing to be closer to his body.

"I want to look at you," he breathes down my back, and I shiver when his breath hits my spine.

He's playing me like an instrument, and I am putty in his hands. He splays his fingers across my skin and I rock my ass back into him. He's already rock hard and I can't help the little whimper of desire that escapes me. I'm ready to do anything he orders me to.

His fingers slide down my neck, tangling in my hair and pulling my head back, and I gasp out loud. They continue their journey down my spine, stopping to rest above my ass cheeks. I'm breathing heavily, I want him so fucking badly. I need him to shove inside me, come home to me. And I'm really damn close to begging.

"Nate..." I whisper.

He doesn't wait for me to continue.

The sound of his slap on my ass reverberates through the echo-y laundry room, and I shiver under his touch. I cry out with delight and surprise.

"I love making your ass blush," Nate whispers in my ear, making my cheeks go red, too.

I like this way too much. "Do it again," I whisper.

He gently caresses my reddening ass cheek, his touch whisper soft on the bare skin. I brace, waiting for the sting of pleasure.

But he only gives me a gentle tap that hardly makes a sound.

It is then that I decide I've had enough.

Yes, he is extremely handsome.

Yes, he is successful.

Yes, he is my boss.

But I know how to play rough too.

And I like it.

I turn around swiftly, blocking access to my ass, and Nate manages to hide his surprise pretty well.

"Strip," I order him, crossing my arms under my breasts.

He gives me a pointed look, that smirk still plastered on his face, but at least he doesn't object. He peels off his shirt first, letting me get a good view of his hard abs.

The sweats follow next, ending up in a heap on the floor. He toys with the waistband of his Calvin Klein boxers until I've finally had enough.

I step closer and pull them down for him.

Good lord, he's magnificent. My own body reacts with lust, the insides of my thighs going damp.

But I'm not going to rush this.

Slowly, I lower myself to my knees, bringing his boxers down to the ground with me. I look up at him, my own cocky smile filling my face as he real-izes what I am about to do. The look of surprise, lust, and adoration on his face fills me with excitement.

"Ada…" He gasps as I trail one finger along his length from base to tip. He throbs in response to my touch.

I repeat the motion, only this time I use the tip of my tongue, leaving a long wet streak on his skin. I blow on it, knowing that the sudden coldness will shock him.

His entire body shudders and I watch as the muscles in his stomach tighten and flex. I look up at him, enjoying the look on his face as I bring my lips to his cock and slowly, so slowly that I know it's driving him absolutely crazy, wrap my mouth around him.

He shudders, reaching out to brace himself against the wall.

"Ada…" He says my name like a grateful prayer.

I use my tongue to swirl, my lips to suck, and my teeth to tease. I feel him harden, growing still wider and longer in my mouth. The small groans and intakes of breath tell me when I do something right, something that I should repeat.

His hands tangle in my hair as his hips start to rock. I wonder if I can get him off like this. I don't want him to come like this, I want to have him inside me, but the idea that I might be able to pleasure him with my mouth and hands to climax is tempting.

I lick him again, from stem to tip, loving the way his stomach muscles tighten.

His grip in my hair tightens and he pulls me away from him, tugging hard enough on my hair to command but not hurt. I stand, following his silent guidance. He kisses me, his tongue finding mine and tangling. His cock presses against me, throbbing slightly in time with our kiss.

I want to feel him inside of me so badly my entire body aches.

I look up at him, a question in my eyes. I glance at his fallen pants, hoping that he is prepared for this moment.

He darts for his pants, finding the pocket and pulling out a foil wrapped square. Before he can tear it open, I take it from him, grinning like a cat who just found the cream.

My hands slide down his chest, his skin smooth and muscles hard beneath my tough. I swallow, suddenly nervous as I reach for him. I shouldn't be, I just sucked on him, but something about touching him, moving him to where I want, feels more intimate.

I caress his hard length in my fingers, loving the way his breath hitches with pleasure at my touch. I feel like a sex goddess to give him pleasure like that. I slide the condom on him, my hands shaking with desire that I can barely control.

He lets go of my hair, his hand sliding down my side and cupping one ass cheek. I groan slightly and he slaps it, the sound ringing through the space.

I raise my leg, and he slides his hand to my thigh, holding it up. My hands maneuver him to my entrance. I look up at him, suddenly shy and a little unsure. All he has to do is thrust his hips and he'll fill me.

He takes his free hand and gently tucks a strand of hair behind my ear before kissing me gently. The motion of his body is slow, but confident. He lets me guide him into me, taking his time as he breaches me for the first time.

I gasp and he groans, lowering his head to place his forehead in the crook of my neck.

"God, you feel so good," he gasps, his hand tightening on my thigh. "How can you possibly feel this good?"

He undulates his hips, moving in and out of me with a rhythm that has my heart racing. Every thrust, every slide into my depths increases the pleasure slowly building deep in my core. He's slowly building to a crescendo that I fear will destroy the universe with the sheer pleasure he is creating inside of me.

I'm going to come undone.

Usually, this takes a lot longer. Usually, it requires more foreplay and a lot more effort from me, but there is just something so primal about the way Nate feels inside of me that the ties that bind me to this earth are coming undone quicker than ever before.

My body tenses, my legs shaking as my core tightens to an unbearable shiver that washes over me with heavenly pleasure and relief.

"Do it again," Nate whispers in my ear.

I whimper as he thrusts hard and fast and I come over the edge again. I cry out in surprise as sweet heaven floods my body, both at his movement and his command for me to do so.

I'm dizzy with pleasure as he picks me up, grabbing both ass cheeks in his hands, and then setting me down on the top of the broken dryer.

He slides back into me and my head falls back, my body still tingling with pleasure from the two orgasams still reverberating through me.

Every thrust has my core tightening again. I wrap my legs around his waist, wanting him to stay deep inside of me yet craving the next thrust more. His hands grip my hips, his breath starting to come in short gasps.

I can feel his muscles tense. I breathe in the scent of his pine scent and coffee as he tips his head, closing his eyes and reveling in the pleasure we both find inside one another. He kisses me, the need within him spilling out in the kiss and filling me with so much desire I'm afraid I might spontaneously explode.

"Come for me," I command, catching his earlobe with my teeth after I say the words.

His entire body goes still for a second, rigid and tense. Then I can feel his pleasure washing through him, I can feel his muscles contract and loosen, and his breath catch as he finally gives into me.

I revel in his pleasure. I focus on the way his ass is tightening, the little crease in his brow, the opening of his mouth as he loses himself to me.

For this moment, he is mine and mine alone.

I didn't know how much I wanted this. I didn't know that it could feel this good to be with someone. I didn't know how his pleasure could magnify and increase my own.

And all I want now is for this moment to never end. I want to feel this little moment of heaven for the rest of my days.

And for just a second, I let myself believe that we could.

 ate

I've never had sex like this.

It's always been calm, collected and calculated. The three C's, Katy used to call it. I thought it was the best way to do things. But right now I could name a thousand things wrong with the three C's.

Because sex isn't supposed to be any of those three things. And it isn't, not with Ada.

It's unpredictable. I mean, we're in my laundry room! Not the most romantic of places.

It's messy. It's dirty. It's oh so good.

She's breathing hard, her skin sticky against mine. I never want this moment to end, because I know what's going to happen when it does.

I'm going to panic.

I'm going to try to run once again. To escape.

I wait for the pressure to become unbearable, the itch to run to take over, the fear to consume me.

But strangely, it doesn't happen. I just feel peace with Ada. I get a towel and pass one to Ada as well, and we grin at each other as we wipe ourselves clean.

"You want to jump in the shower?" I surprise myself by asking. Usually, I'd be wanting to get her the hell out of my apartment as soon as possible.

Well, scratch that. Usually, none of my conquests even end up in my apartment. So far, that has been a privilege reserved only for Katy. I don't let people get close.

"Again?" Ada asks me with a silly smile.

"Yep," I reply seriously, smacking her ass on my way to the bathroom. "Come in here. It'll feel good, I promise."

She follows me, heading into the bathroom and closing the door behind us. I turn on the shower, making the water get nice and hot for us, and I get in with Ada.

Her young body is toned and sexy as hell, and in mere moments, my hands are roaming down her back once more.

"I can't resist you," I murmur against her ear.

I don't think she can hear me over the sound of the water, and I'm glad of it. I don't often like to show how vulnerable I can get, and even though I like Ada, I don't completely trust her with my weaknesses - not just yet.

My hands slide over Ada's hot skin, feeling the curves of her body. She groans as I reach for a bottle of body wash, squeezing out a good amount. I lather us both up, and the fresh smell of crisp red apple envelops the whole shower. I inhale it, letting it settle deep down. It's a scent I'll connect with Ada from now on.

My hands linger on her smooth skin. She's flawless to my eyes, every freckle and every mole making her more perfect. Her hands skim my shoulders, tracing the lines of my muscles. She rubs shampoo into my hair, massaging my scalp. It's better than any haircut place.

I revel in the gentle touch of her fingers. This shower is intimate and romantic. It's sexy as hell, and I'm hard as a rock, but there's no need for sex. I kiss her neck, inhaling the soft fragrance of her wet skin. The soap lets my fingers slide across her curves, her hips, her breasts.

She giggles, pushing my hair up into what I assume is a mohawk. She giggles again, this time making my hair look like Elvis. It feels so good that I don't mind. Besides, her giggles are a balm to my soul. How could anyone feel the slightest bit of stress when that sound is around?

For the first time in months, I can feel my shoulders relaxing. I could let Ada in. I could let her be a part of my life. I could have this every day.

And something about that terrifies me.

"You okay?" she asks, pulling away her soap filled hands. Her eyes are full of concern and I realize that I've frozen. My muscles have tensed and I've pulled away from her.

I force a smile. "I'm fine," I tell her. "We're just going to run out of hot water soon."

Her body relaxes again. "Then let me rinse your hair," she says, reaching for me again.

I try not to tense, but I don't know how to be relaxed anymore. I let out a long breath, trying to rinse away my anxiety along with the shampoo bubbles. It seems to work and I feel better as I watch the soap swirl the drain.

By the time we're finally done, the water is running

cold and we're shivering. We get out of the shower and I dry us both of with a big, fluffy white towel. Ada smiles at me shyly as we pull our clothes back on in the laundry room. I love seeing her in my things.

"Hey," I say on a whim. "Do you wanna sleep over?"

Ada seems surprised by my question, and I hate it. Hate that she thinks I wouldn't ask her that. It's a normal thing to do, right? Ask your lover to stay the night.

I guess the painful thing is, I don't do this. Ever.

Yeah, I've slept with girls before - and after - Katy. But I don't ever invite them to sleep over. In fact, I never even bring them back to my place. I keep everyone at a distance.

"Yeah, okay," she says with a small smile.

If I had any doubts about asking her to stay over, they dissipate when I see how happy Ada is. And I'm happy too. My life finally looks like it might be changing for the better.

"What're we gonna do with the pup?" Ada asks me.

We both look in the direction of the dog, curled up on the couch.

"I guess we could put him in the bedroom," I groan. "Just so he doesn't piss all over my carpet."

"Nathaniel Rhodes," Ada pokes me playfully. "You're warming up to the little critter, aren't you?"

"Shut up," I say, shaking my head and laughing.

I pick up the dog along with the blanket and turn off the lights. We head into my bedroom, my favorite place in the whole apartment. It's enormous, and in the center, there's a bed big enough for several people to sleep in.

Of course, they never do.

It's always just me.

Lonely old me.

I deposit the pup at the foot of the bed, and Ada and I curl up against the headboard.

"Hey," she says softly so as not to disturb the snoring dog. "What are you calling him? The dog?"

"Nate. That way I won't forget his name," I say immediately, and we both laugh quietly.

"Seriously," Ada says.

"Well, why don't you pick a name?" I suggest. "You are the one who found him, after all."

"Alright," she drawls, thinking hard.

Her forehead creases as she ponders the dog's name, and it's the cutest thing I've ever seen. I can't help myself, I lean over to her and kiss her long and hard. Fuck, this girl is driving me crazy.

"I like Rocky," she finally says.

"Rocky?" I repeat. "Like the fighter?"

She shrugs. "Yes, but that's not what I'm referencing. Your last name is Rhodes, and he should have your last name."

Rocky Rhodes.

"Like the ice cream. I like it." I kiss her on the forehead. "Rocky it is."

We settle in the bed and I cover us up with a blanket. So far, there hasn't been a single word about the next day. We're going to have to head to work together, and I'm kind of nervous about that. I have problems making my relationships public like that, probably because I'm wary after what happened with Katy.

"Good night, Nate," Ada tells me softly. She kisses my cheek, feather soft and wonderful.

Her eyes are already closed and she's turned on her

side, facing me. I pull her closer and she hugs me back, not too tight. A small smile is playing on her lips and it's the sweetest thing I've seen all day.

"Good night, Ada," I say.

I drift off to sleep moments later.

ate

I wake up from a nightmare hours later, drenched in sweat and panting.

I don't scream. I don't startle. I just open my eyes and realize it was a dream.

Thank god. It was just a nightmare.

It's already light outside, even though the days are slowly but surely getting shorter. I look at my alarm clock on the bedside table and realize it's barely five in the morning.

I look over to Ada's side of the bed. She's curled up in a little ball, sleeping soundly.

A little yelp moves my attention away from my employee and to the furry little ball at my feet.

Rocky is sitting down next to the bed, wagging his tail like crazy and giving me a sideways look.

A quick inspection of the room doesn't reveal a single puddle or poop, and I realize he really must be itching to get out of here.

I guess this is my life now, I realize silently, as I get up and scoop Rocky up in my arms. I'll have to get a leash and some other dog stuff today. Maybe I could take Ada shopping with me, or is that taking it too far?

I laugh at myself. Too far? I just slept with the girl. Too far was hours ago.

The sun is still tucked nice and deep under the horizon. It will be autumn soon, and I can feel the cool of it coming before the sun rises. Fall. The students are back in session. The leaves are still green, but patches of yellow are starting to poke out of branches and Halloween decorations are already starting to show up.

I need to come up with my caramel coffee. Or pumpkin spice. Or apple cinnamon. Something to take advantage of the fall weather. But I have no ideas and my brain is skittering around like an ice cube dropped on the floor. I can't seem to settle and I have more energy than I should.

I take Rocky to the small back yard behind the coffee shop. It's not much of a yard, and it usually ends up being extra storage space for equipment, but there's a little grass and a small bush.

I'm already starting to come up with ideas on how to make it a puppy paradise. That at least captures my attention for a few moments, but as soon as Rocky is done with his business, I'm drowning in my thoughts again.

I carefully bring him back upstairs. Ada is still sleeping, her soft snores loud in the quiet of my home. It feels strange to have someone else here. Rocky settles on the floor with a contented sigh, obviously all tuckered out and ready for another nap.

I'm feeling antsy and edgy, although I can't seem to put my finger on why. I pace my kitchen for a moment, deciding if I should brew us a pot of coffee.

Although, why brew a pot when I can just run downstairs and get lattes and donuts. Besides, the coffee pot would make noise and I don't want to wake her when she looks so peaceful.

"You just need some food," I tell myself, ignoring the tightening in my chest.

Downstairs, I grab a bunch of donuts and some bear claws for Ada and me, even managing to grab two lattes without Sydney saying anything. I head back through the kitchen, past my office. As I pass the door to the office and open the door that leads to the stairs, my phone rings.

I glance down at the number and immediately pick up. "Hello."

"Is this Nathaniel Rhodes?" a female voice asks.

"Yes." My throat closes up and I can't say more than that single word.

"There's been an incident. We're calling to inform you that–"

"Is he okay?" I interrupt. I set the donuts down on my desk.

"Yes." The woman sounds flustered which only makes me more nervous. "We caught him before he left the grounds, but he did sustain some minor injuries and he assaulted one of the nurses."

"Is the nurse okay?" I close my eyes, forcing myself to breathe.

"Yes. She only sustained minor injuries, but it could

have been more serious. We understand the nature of his condition, but it is concerning. If this occurs again, you will have to find a new facility."

In and out. Just breathe in and out. It doesn't matter that there are no other facilities that can take him.

"Sir?" The woman cuts into my mediation. "We're going to need you to come and sign some paperwork."

"I'll be there as soon as I can."

I hang up the phone and stare at it. A sob wells up from the pit of my stomach. I didn't ask for this. I don't want this fate.

WIthout thinking, I chuck my phone as hard as I can at the cement floor. A sick part of me revels in the destruction, watching the screen shatter.

And then I realize that was a stupid thing to do. Something my father would do. Yet one more way I am becoming like him. Yet one more way that my fate will be the same as his.

"Are you okay back there?" Sydney shouts from the kitchen. I see her head poking out into the hallway, a frown on her face.

"I'm fine. Just tripped," I mutter, and she gives me one last worried look before carrying on with her life. The café is busy and she doesn't have time for me if I say I'm fine.

I stare at the broken phone on the floor, feeling like a complete and total idiot. I'm better than this. I refuse to end up like him, even if my genetics say otherwise. My fate is coming for me and there is nothing I can do to stop it.

My hands shake as I climb the stairs to my home. My

feet are lead. It's hard to breathe, but I open the door and go inside.

I deposit the two coffees on the counter. A memory of my father bringing me coffee like this fills my mind. He'd used salt instead of sugar. I'd laughed, but he'd been so angry. It had been a warning sign of what was coming, one that I'd missed. I'd simply passed it off as a simple mistake.

The what if's begin to echo through my brain. What if I did that to Ada? What if I followed my father? What if…

Panic washes over me. I can't do this to her. I can't let her live in this hell that I share with my father. With a painful jab to my heart, I realize I need to leave. I need to get out of here. I need to escape this place.

I scramble to find a piece of paper and a pen, and my hands shake as I write down a note to Ada. I feel like the world's biggest coward, just walking out on her like this. I'm a jackass, but I can't help myself. I need to get away from her to protect her.

I look at the pathetic piece of paper I've torn from a notebook.

Good morning. Here's some coffee for you - promise it's not caramel. I'll see you at work.

- Nathaniel

I feel shitty as fuck for walking out on Ada. I should wait for her to wake up, maybe explain the situation, but then I'd have to explain everything.

I can't put this on her. She's so young. She deserves so much more than someone like me.

Coffee in hand, I walk outside. I'm too worried to simply go to my office, and cowardly know that Ada would check for me there. I can't go to the facility yet. I need to calm down first. I go toward the Main Street Park which is relatively close to Perk Me Up. It's our local city park with walking paths, trees, and the ability to imagine I am alone in nature.

I walk the paths until my feet are screaming and tired and the sun is already high up in the sky. I watch small kids play with their mothers on the swings. I watch the ducks and geese float lazily around the lake. Two college kids play frisbee in one of the fields, but I don't want to join them.

I should go back to work, but my feet stay rooted to the cement under the park bench. My stomach growls, but I ignore it. I remember my father. I think of all the things Ada can do without me and my weight dragging her down.

I wish I hadn't smashed my phone, because I need to talk to Ada, even though I don't know what to say. How do I tell her that I'm no good for her? I sit in the park doing absolutely nothing, because at the end of the day, I know that I will be nothing but a burden to her.

I finally make the drive to the facility. I sign the paper-work, and apologize to the nurse. Her kindness and understanding of the situation only makes it worse. I would prefer her to be angry, not merciful. I can manage anger, but her gentle acceptance makes my own fate loom larger.

Soon it will be me that needs that mercy.

I drive home in the dark, grateful for the dark shadows that hide my arrival to the shop. I take the back entrance, slipping up the stairs without anyone seeing me. When only Rocky greets me, I don't know whether the empty feeling in my stomach is relief, or regret.

da

I guess I've been dumped.

It shouldn't be a big deal - God knows it's happened plenty of times before. But I could always pinpoint it to a reason. Maybe I was too clingy. Too aloof. Too eager. Too boring. We just didn't click.

Not this time, not with Nathaniel.

As soon as I saw the note he'd left me in the kitchen along with the coffee but nothing else, I knew he wanted me to pretend like nothing had ever happened between us.

I held the note in trembling hands, seeing it for what it was: a dismissal. He'd gotten his notch on the bedpost and he was done with me. I'm surprised he let me stay the night, but then again, I'd performed well and it was raining out.

I toss it in the trash. I deserve better than cold coffee and an empty bed.

I pet Rocky. He's happily curled up on a blanket near the fireplace. There is no fire, no sign of life. I make sure that he has a bowl of fresh water and that he can't get into too much mischief until Nathaniel decides to come home.

I keep my head held high as I walk past his office on my way out the back. He's not there. There's not even an empty coffee cup on his desk to show he was there at all today. The small hope that he'd just let me sleep in and gone to work evaporated. He wasn't there. He wasn't out in the front helping Sydney. Of course, I bet he's found a safer place to hide from me.

I make a promise to myself to do my damn best to not show any emotion around him. If he doesn't want to take this any further, I'm going to take the damn high road. I can be a bigger person. I can be the mature one.

I try to convince myself I regret the previous evening on my way home from Nate's apartment. I try to convince myself that I didn't feel anything. That the electric connection between us was all in my head. That I don't want him to find me and apologize and tell me that he loves me.

I bite my lower lip, feeling confused and upset. I don't get why he just pushed me away like that. Maybe I got too close in a too-short amount of time...

He's older than me. He has a life and responsibilities that I don't. Maybe he just sees me as a dumb kid. I wish I knew why he didn't want me, because the rejection hurts more than I want to admit. But it won't do me any good to dwell on Nate's state of mind or the reasons behind his actions. The best thing to do here is to forget, and to move on.

Back in my apartment, I take a quick shower and wash off last night. As painful as it is, I need to move on. It's obvious this was merely a one night stand for Nathaniel. Too bad it meant more to me.

I know I have to head back to work today, and the knowledge is killing me. While Nate didn't outright say he didn't want to see me again, I have a sinking feeling things between us are going to be awkward as hell. I have no idea what to even say to him.

I spend the first half of the day sulking in my apartment and watching trashy reality shows. Once the time to leave for work finally comes, I'm annoyed and nervous as hell. For the first time ever since I started working at Perk Me Up, I'm late.

Sydney seems mildly annoyed when I walk into Perk Me Up, but as soon as she sees my expression, she seems to realize something is wrong. I guess I give off an I-don't-want-to-talk-about-it vibe though, as she doesn't question me about what's wrong once.

She does, however, buy me a pain au raisin for lunch, and I smile gratefully when she slides it over to me across the counter. I keep busy, finding things to occupy my hands and mind. When I'm not making coffee, I clean everything I can get my hands on.

The napkin holders have never been so shiny.

I don't see Nate for the whole day. There's no texts or missed calls. Nothing. I guess it's better that way. But there's no denying the dull pain in my chest, which worsens even more when he doesn't show up to help lock up.

~

The next week or so goes by in a hurry. I work, and I'm getting ready for school to start any moment now. I've gotten most of my textbooks, and I'm pretty excited about some of the classes I've decided to take this fall.

I hang out with Jacob and the rest of the gang pretty much every day, and they help me take my mind off of things. But I don't tell anyone about Nate and me. I keep that heartache to myself.

That is, until the first shift I share with Layla that week, the last lazy Thursday afternoon before classes start. As soon as she walks into Perk Me Up, she seems to know something is off, and she gives me a worried look as she puts on her apron.

It's not a busy day, and a few hours later, we take a small break, making ourselves some lattes and sitting down at the counter. Students trickle in, but without classes to study for, most people are making good use of the warm weather outside.

"Spill the beans," Layla orders me without further ado.

I give her a long, inquisitive look. There's two ways to go about this. I can either deny there's something amiss, or do as she asked and tell her exactly what's bothering me.

And I know what's going to happen before I even open my mouth. Layla just has that trustworthy air about her, and I feel like I can trust her with my secrets, even though she seems pretty close to Nathaniel.

I tell her everything.

My words start slow, but quickly gain speed. I tell her

about our flirting, about the night we spent together in Nate's apartment. Layla's eyes widen when I tell her I've been to his place, and I briefly wonder if she even knows where he lives. Surely she must, they seem to be pretty great friends.

I'm itching to ask about Rocky, see how he is doing. I've always been a big animal person, even though my parents never let me have any pets. I've always wanted a dog and I miss the little guy.

"So I guess I'm just a little miffed," I finish by saying. "I thought he would be... nicer after the night we spent together. I really feel like we connected."

"So do I," Layla admits out loud. She sips thoughtfully on her coffee. "Do you want me to ask him about it?"

"Hell no," I reply with a nervous chuckle. "Don't even mention it to him. Best to just move on, pretend like nothing out of the ordinary happened."

I fidget in my seat, warming my palms on the steaming cup of coffee.

"Hey, I haven't really seen Nate around, though," I admit. "Maybe just tell him I'm cool and it's ok to come to work. I promise I won't make a scene. No coffee will be thrown. In fact, I promise not to throw anything at all."

I'm trying to joke about the whole thing, but the fact of the matter is, Nathaniel Rhodes has been avoiding me, and it hurts. He has only been in the office when I'm not scheduled. Sydney has seen him, but he seems to have mysterious errands he has to run just as I arrive or he locks himself in the office. As much as I wish I could say I want to take that night back, I can't bring myself to do it.

"I will tell him that you promise not to throw anything

at him or make a scene," Layla replies. She sets down her coffee. "But I can't guarantee that I won't. He deserves to have a little coffee thrown at his head over this. We should get back to work."

I smile, but it doesn't really touch my eyes.

da

I wake up to a psychotically cheerful beeping sound right next to my head. It's still pitch black out, so I know it's not my alarm. With a groan, I pick up my phone and frown at the number flashing across the screen. Who on earth could be calling me at three in the morning?

My eyes are blurry with sleep and my mind just as groggy as I fumble for the phone. I struggle to slide the answer button in my half-asleep fugue.

"Hello?" I croak, sleep heavy in my voice.

"Ada?"

The voice on the other end of the line is panicked. It's also deep and masculine and completely, uncharacteristically, scared.

Nathaniel.

"Yes?" I reply in a clipped tone. I'm very awake now.

If this is a fucking booty call, so help me God, I will beat the shit out of him.

"Can you come over?" he asks in that same panicked, worried tone.

I'm about to launch into a speech about where he can go if he thinks I"ll jump when he calls, when he adds something that changes everything.

"It's Rocky," he says softly. "I think something's wrong."

I don't think twice before answering, "I'll be there in fifteen."

My mind is clearer as I get up, taking off my PJs and pulling on some yoga pants and a simple T-shirt. A hoodie goes over my head next and I grab my keys before locking my apartment.

I move quietly, hurting out into the dark night. There's a cool hint of autumn coming and the scent of moisture in the air. I shiver slightly, wrapping my arms around my middle. Luckily, this is a college town and the school prides themselves on keeping the place safe.

I start jogging, not because I'm cold, but because I'm worried. How bad does Rocky have to be in order for Nate to call me?

Truth be told, I'm still regretting not putting my foot down and asking Nate for me to be the one that kept him.

My jog to Perk Me Up is quick and uneventful, and I thankfully don't run into any sketchy characters. I hurry around the back, going to the employee entrance. I punch in my code and the buzzer lets me in.

A bewildered, pale as fuck Nate greets me at the bottom of the stairs.

Or rather, runs towards me and gives me a tight hug.

"Thank you for coming," he tells me. "Thank you so fucking much."

He smells so damn good. Pine trees and dark coffee. I could drink him in and I find myself breathing in the scent of him without thinking. I love the way I feel in his arms, even though I shouldn't.

Feeling confused and overwhelmed, I gently push him away, and give him a long look. Now is not the time to question what happened between us. First, I need to know what's wrong.

"Where's Rocky?" I ask, trying hard to keep my voice strong and steady.

Nate takes my hand, sending hot flashes over my whole body. He gently pulls me to his office where he has Nate in a little doggy bed.

As soon as I see the sandy-colored pup, I know something's off. The usually energetic and happy, tail-wagging dog seems off, lying on his side and whimpering softly, barely keeping his eyes open.

"We need to go to a vet," I say right away, and Nate nods.

"Everything's closed," he tells me in a panicked voice. "I've called everyone. Every-fucking-one, every office in the town, and no one will take us... The nearest emergency vet is two hours away, and I'm worried he'll... it'll take too long."

We exchange a long worried glance.

"We can call Audrey," I tell him. "She's studying to be a vet. I think it's pretty much the best thing we can do right now."

"Your friend?" Nathaniel asks in a shaky voice. I hate

that I want to wrap him up in my arms and tell him that everything is going to be okay.

I nod, already pulling out my phone and dialing my best friend's number. I'm going to pay for this one - I know Audrey claims she needs at least six hours of sleep, and I know for a fact she went to bed late - she had a date just hours prior.

She picks up on the second ring, and Nate stares at me with wide, scared eyes as I fill her in on what's going on.

Audrey is a trooper just like always, and she agrees to come to Perk Me Up right away. I can tell she's a little bit annoyed when we start talking, but she turns professional and sweet at the same time as soon as I mention there's an animal in distress.

I hear someone else's voice in the background, which leads me to believe her date went well. I end the call with a small smile.

"She'll be here in twenty minutes," I tell Nate.

"Oh, thank fuck." He runs his fingers through that dark flop of hair, which looks messy at this time of the night. "Thank you so much, Ada. I don't know what I would've done without you."

"Don't mention it," I reply, kneeling down next to the puppy.

Rocky looks weak, and I pet him gently to make him feel a little bit better. He gets up on shaky little legs, and throws up all over the floor.

"Jesus," Nate says in a panicked tone, pacing the room. "Fuck, fuck, fuck. What are we gonna do? What if something happens to him? What if he...?"

"Calm down," I tell him, gently lifting the pup back onto his bed.

He's breathing a little more evenly now, which makes me feel a bit better.

"Just get me a mop and some disinfectant," I tell Nate. "We need to get this place clean. And get a rag, run it under cold water for Rocky."

It seems to help Nate to have something to do, and he rushes into the kitchen to do what I told him. I gently stroke Rocky's belly while Nate is gone, noticing it's a little swollen. But the pup looks better now, he's breathing more evenly and his breaths are less ragged.

Once Nate returns, I drape the cool cloth over Rocky, covering him with it. He seems to calm down once I lay it on him, and I'll bet it feels good on his scorching hot belly.

Nate scrubs the vomit off the floor, and I try to get Rocky to drink some water. He takes a few laps at the bowl in front of him, which I take to be a good sign. I'll take anything at this point. I know Nate is worried, but fear is eating me up from the inside, too.

We don't speak much, instead kneeling down next to the doggy bed. I don't expect Nate to apologize, not at all. I think there's something going on with him, something I might not quite understand. I want to believe that we've just had some kind of horrible miscommunication.

The waves of self-doubt and worry are coming off my boss in waves, and he's pacing the room, running his fingers through his wild mop of hair, and cursing softly. His cool confidence is gone, and I can suddenly see the age of him. He's not old, but he's tired.

At one point, when we're both crouched down next to Rocky, I feel Nate's hand in mine. He reaches over and holds me softly, perhaps a way to say I'm sorry and thank you in one.

I can feel his eyes on me, but I'm too fucking tired to return his hopeful gaze. Instead, I gently stroke his hand with my thumb, and he squeezes me.

Audrey calls me and I run to the front door to let her in. She walks to the office, looking tired but collected at the same time.

"Hey, guys," she says softly. "Where's our patient?"

We show her Rocky, giving her some space and letting her get some work down. She gets on her hands and knees, taking the dog's temperature, feeling his belly, and stroking his sandy fur.

Finally, she gets up minutes later, and gives us a long look.

"He ate something," she tells us. "He must've found something on the street that was bad."

"But I've been keeping such a close eye on him," Nate rattles, looking panicked. "I mean, I always watch out..."

"Has anyone else been walking him?" Audrey interrupts him.

Nate thinks for a moment before replying, "Just once. My..."

Nate looks at me, and I give him a blank look.

"My friend walked him."

Oh, I see what he means. A *friend*. Sure.

Jackass. I take a step away from him.

"Once is enough," Audrey tells him with a regretful smile. "The good news is, Rocky will be perfectly alright."

I breathe a sigh of relief, forgetting to be mad at Nathaniel for a short moment, and my boss envelops Audrey in a huge hug.

"Are you sure?" I ask her.

She pats Nate on the back awkwardly, giving me a weird look over his shoulder. I roll my eyes in response. She knows I slept with Nate and then that he ghosted me, so I'm sure she's as confused as I am about finding me here in the middle of the night.

"Yes," she says once Nate finally lets go. "He'll probably vomit a couple more times, but whatever it was, he didn't eat enough of it to cause any serious damage."

"Thank you so much," Nate gushes. "I don't know how I can ever repay you."

"Free coffee for the rest of my life?" Audrey jokes.

"You got it," Nate replies with a solemn nod, and my friend and I exchange another surprised look.

"Anyway," Audrey says to break up the awkwardness. "I'll be on my way. Keep him cool and make sure he drinks a lot, and he should be fine in a couple of hours."

"I'll come with you," I nod at her as she grabs her jacket. "We can walk together."

"Wait."

I turn around to face Nate. He looks a little better now, but his under-eye circles are bright blue and he still looks like hell. At least the panic-stricken pain is gone from his face.

"Can you please wait a moment, Ada?" he asks me softly.

"I need to sleep," I reply monotonously, while Audrey does her best to turn invisible.

"Please." Nate's voice is small, almost vulnerable. "I'll pay for a cab back to your place."

I look at the floor, knowing full-well I should tell him to go to hell. But in the end, I'm so fucking hopeful he'll apologize, I give him a curt nod and hug Audrey goodbye.

"I'll see you tomorrow," I tell her.

"Yep, I'll be in Perk Me Up at eleven."

She hugs me, and I'm thankful as ever she doesn't mention how awkward this whole situation is. Audrey waves goodbye to Nate, and leaves us alone in Nate's office, the bells above the door ringing solemnly as she exits the store.

I stand there with my arms crossed as Nate approaches me. I'm looking at the ceiling, the hallway, Rocky - anything but Nate's eyes.

"Ada," he says.

I still can't look at him.

"Ada, please."

I can't do it. I'm worried I'll fucking break if I look him in the eye.

Because I know it was a one night stand.

I know it didn't mean anything to him.

I know I'm just a conquest.

I know he's gonna give me a bullshit apology, and I'll only feel worse after.

Because for me, it was so much more than that.

Because sometimes, a single night can mean so much more.

I feel Nate's hands on my face, and he gently tips my chin back, forcing me to look at him.

"Please," he says again."I want to apologize."

"No need," I reply in a clipped tone, but I can't seem to pull away from his touch. "No hard feelings at all, Nathaniel."

"I've been a dick," he replies, ignoring my comment.

"Yes. Yes, you have." This time, I pull away from him, missing the warmth of his fingers on my chin.

Nathaniel laughs, a soft, calming sound that gives me butterflies. Fuck him, and what he still does to my body. My body aches to have him fill me again. To have his touch on my skin and the way he sets my nerves on pleasurable fire.

"I..." he starts again, sighing and running his hands through his hair, something I'm quickly realizing is kind of a nervous tick for him. "I fucked up. I got scared. I don't like letting people get too close. I'm worried they'll find out too much about me."

"I wasn't trying to break down your walls," I tell him quietly. "I was just trying to get to know you."

"I guess I'm worried it will still happen," he chokes out. "The moment you see who I really am, the walls will come down. And then I won't just be Nathaniel Rhodes, a successful businessman. I'll be a fucking failure, and all you'll feel is contempt for me. You deserve someone better than me, Ada."

"Oh, Nate." I look at him with surprise in my eyes. So there is something more to the whole story. He seems quite shaken up, and I realize admitting all of that took quite a lot of effort for Nate.

"My father..." He pauses, taking a breath. "I don't want to hurt you. I don't want to cause you pain that you don't deserve."

I wonder what his father did to scar Nate into pushing people away.

"I don't want to make you uncomfortable," I tell him. "I just... don't like being pushed away. But I'm glad you called me tonight. I'm glad I could help."

"Thank you so much for coming," he gushes. "I'm so fucking grateful, Ada, you've no idea..."

"It's ok," I say with a smile, some of my anger ebbing. "Look, let's just... move on. Move past this."

With a huge smile, Nate moves in closer to me, his hands going to my hips. My heartbeat immediately picks up, beating faster than ever. I want to kiss him. I want to run my hands all over his skin and feel every inch of him.

But I gently push him away.

"No," I whisper. My heart doesn't want to say the words, but I have to protect myself. "I can't do it that way. You're too hot and cold. It makes me... it fucks with my head."

Nate stares at me for a long time, and a mix of feelings are displayed on his face. Longing. Heartache. Regret.

"I'm sorry," I say, extending a hand for him to shake. I hope he doesn't see how much I'm trembling. "Friends?"

He reaches for it and shakes a moment later, and I can tell he doesn't like it.

"Friends," he repeats.

He doesn't want it, and I can't say that it's what I want either. I want so much more.

CHAPTER 17

$\mathscr{N}$ ate

"I've never had a dog before," I tell Ada, as we watch Rocky sleep.

Ada is curled up on the couch, wrapped up in a soft knitted blanket with a mug in her hands. She's as far away from me as she can get without being in a different room.

"No?" She looks surprised. "Was someone in your family allergic?"

I shake my head. "No. Just too busy. My parents were professors here at the school."

She nods, taking a sip from her mug. It's herbal tea, not coffee.

"What did they teach?" she asks.

"My dad taught math," I reply. "My mom was his grad student."

"Ah, so dating younger women runs in the family," she teases. Her eyes go wide, as if she just realized what she's said. "Sorry. I don't mean…"

"No, it's fine," I tell her. "She adored him. She thought he was the smartest person on the planet."

I remember the way she used to look at him, like he hung the moon in the sky. There was always a softness, even when she knew he was wrong. She'd hate what he'd become. I was glad she wasn't around to see what was happening to him now.

"Sounds romantic," Ada says, sipping at her tea again.

"My mom used to host these elaborate dinner parties," I say, closing my eyes and remembering. "My father loved them. I was even allowed to participate as long as I behaved. I'd forgotten how much she liked to cook."

"They sound wonderful. Do they come to visit often?" Ada asks.

"My mom died ten years ago." There's no emotion in my voice. "It was a ruptured brain aneurysm. She fell on some ice and then just didn't wake up the next morning."

"Oh. I'm so sorry." Ada's voice is small. "And your dad?"

I don't want to talk about my dad, so I change the subject. "Do you think Rocky is warm enough?"

"I think he's fine," Ada replies, looking over at the sleeping puppy. "He looks pretty comfortable."

We both watched him for a moment. His breathing is better and his stomach looks more comfortable.

Ada doesn't ask me about my parents again. She changes the subject to her classes, rambling on about how she's learning to shoot corporate photos and how the lighting really matters. It's safe territory for both of us.

A big weight falls off my shoulders when Rocky finally gets up and licks my hand. I've gotten attached to the pup, more than I ever thought I would, and seeing him in pain made me ache.

By the time six a.m. rolls around, Rocky is happily munching on some chicken and rice, and Ada and I decide he'll be fine. I tell her to go home, and that there's no need to come to work in only a few short hours, but she vehemently shakes her head and tells me she will definitely come in.

Her determination makes my heart ache. She's so loyal. So kind.

I've screwed up royally by pushing her away, and this whole experience with Rocky only served to confirm that. Unfortunately, there's nothing I can do about it save for apologizing, and I've already done that. It seems as if Ada isn't ready to move on from my mistake, as she wants us to be just friends.

I can't say that I blame her. I can't say that she wouldn't be better off without me.

But she was the person I called when I got into trouble. She is the person I want by my side. It may make me a terrible person to do to her what my father would have done to my mother if she had lived, but I can't help myself.

I want Ada in my life. Even if it's selfish.

I put Rocky's leash on and we head downstairs to let him go potty. It's a measure of how much better he's feeling that he happily jumps down the stairs and promptly pees on a bush.

"I'll see you in a few hours," she tells me.

"If you're sure," I reply. "You really don't have to."

We stare at each other in uncomfortable silence, and I'm so terribly desperate for her to touch me. Yet I know she won't, and I know it's too early for me to make a move, too.

"Get some rest, please," I tell her, and she gives me a curt nod.

"Keep an eye on Rocky. Make sure he gets plenty of liquids," she suggests, and I nod before waving her off.

I watch her retreating back, wishing I was brave enough to tell her not to go. Wishing I could explain how much she already means to me, even after the short time we've known each other. But I'm a mess, and she doesn't need to deal with my shit. I've put her through enough already.

I taek Rocky back upstairs and let him snuggle into bed with me. I know that he should sleep on the very comfortable memory foam dog bed at the foot of my bed, but after tonight, I want him close to me.

I lie on my back on my 1200-thread count sheets, with Rocky's head settled on my lap. He sighs contentedly as I stroke his short curly fur, but I'm feeling less than relaxed.

I've been a jackass. I never should've pushed Ada away like that, and I knew that from the get-go. She's such a sweet girl, and she doesn't deserve me treating her that way.

I contemplate everything that's happened for ages, until my alarm beeps with a warning. I have a lot of work today, and I really need to figure out something about the loan. I roll out of bed and head to the office to once again stare at spreadsheets.

Once the clock turns to eleven a.m. and I still haven't figured out any of my problems, I decide I need some serious help. It seems like all I've been doing for the past few days is calling my friends in distress...

I call Layla this time.

She doesn't have a shift today, and I'm sure she's busy with whatever her colorful life has in store for her. Still, I beg her to come see me, and she agrees.

Thirty minutes later, I go to the coffee shop area and smile shyly at Ada, who is standing behind the counter, true to her word. I'd expect nothing less from her.

Layla is already waiting for me at a corner table, leaving me my favorite window seat. She smiles and waves me over, giving me a tight hug before letting me sit down.

"How's the pup?" she asks worriedly.

Today she is wearing a floral dress with a corset top and flared skirt. She's paired it with a leather jacket in pink and biker boots. Her hair is a cotton candy shade of pink. She looks stunning, as always.

"He's much better, thank you," I reply. "Love the hair, by the way."

She touches her locks with her free hand, the other cradling a cup of coffee. Smiling at me, she doesn't say another thing, and I know she's waiting for me to go on.

Ada approaches our table and takes my order, then disappears without another word. Layla catches me staring at her as she leaves, and she whistles.

"This girl again?" she asks me. "What did you do this time?"

I look away guiltily, and she shakes her head. There's not a malicious bone in Layla's body, but that doesn't mean she won't tease me a little for liking Ada.

"You two an item yet?" she wonders out loud, and I shake my head.

"I think I screwed up," I admit in a small voice.

"Well, let's see," Layla says. "You took her out for a date, ignored her for a week, then showed her your apartment, which, so far, only Katy has seen. Then you pushed her away again, and then you called her in the middle of the night to come rescue you and your puppy. And now you're sad about her not being into you."

"Well, it sounds horrible when you say it like that," I tell her.

"Like what, the truth?" Layla teases me, but seeing my fed-up expression, she quickly changes her tone. "What's wrong, Nate? You haven't really been yourself. I know something's wrong."

I give her a long look. I could tell her everything right now, and she wouldn't judge me for it. But I don't want her to pity me, and the moment I open my mouth to speak, I feel like I'm being strangled. Not a single word passes my lips, and all I manage is shaking my head in defeat.

"You don't have to tell me," Layla says, covering my hand with hers.

Ada chooses that moment to arrive with my latte, and we spring apart so she can put it on the table. She gives me a worried look, and I stare back at her for a long moment before she leaves us again.

"You really like her, don't you?" Layla asks me softly.

I give her a pathetic, puppy-eyed look, and she smiles.

"I'll give you a word of sound advice," Layla tells me. "Life is short. Life can be bitter. But if you put just a teaspoon of sugar in your coffee, it might just change your perspective."

She motions towards Ada with her head.

"I think Ada could be the sweetness you need right now, babe."

"I don't know," I sigh.

"What's stopping you, then?" she asks me.

"I don't want to open up." The words leave my mouth before I can stop them.

"Why not?" Layla wants to know.

I hesitate, toying with the hem of my dress shirt.

"Because, I..." I look up at her, finally deciding this is one part of myself I'm ready to reveal to her. After all, she has been my best friend for years. She knows mostly everything about me - including the whole Katy saga. "I opened up to Katy," I finally admit. "And look how that ended. It left me miserable, it got my heart broken. And I'm worried the same will happen with Ada."

Layla leans forward, looking into my eyes.

"Katy was a bitch," she says simply. "You loved her, and she used you. You wanted to make it work, but it never would've happened between the two of you. You were too desperate to make your relationship be something it never would've become."

I look at Layla for a long time, contemplating her words. It's almost scary how right she is.

"Katy will find a guy," she continues. "She'll find a man she'll be able to be there for. She'll be happy with the right person. She won't be the annoyed, snappy and rude girl she became when she was with you, just because she felt guilty for not being the right woman for you. And as for you..." She looks back at Ada, then winks at me. "I think you've already found your woman."

I turn back to stare at Ada, and I know Layla is right. Ada is the one I want."Now you just have to get her back."

ate

Now the only thing left to do is fix things with Ada. And I have a plan for that, too.

I'm going to do something my mother used to do. Something that I'd forgotten that she loved doing for my father.

I have Ada to thank for the idea. She is the one who brought up my mother and made me start thinking of how I am also like her.

I don't have to be my father. Perhaps I can be my mother. I've been convinced that I am going to turn out to be a replica of my father with all his problems and diagnosis, but there is a chance that I am actually more like my mother.

I am going to give that possibility a chance. Ada deserves someone like my mother. She deserves to be with someone that thinks she's the best thing since sliced bread. That is a future that I can get behind. It is one that doesn't fill me with terror.

Rocky and I go to my office to plan. He sleeps peacefully on his dog bed while I spend an hour surfing the web for recipes and making plans. I have a big smile on my face. Finally, it feels like things are about to pick up again.

"Hey, Nathaniel." A familiar voice interrupts my thoughts, and I look up to see Ada fidgeting in my doorway. She's playing with her necklace and chewing on her bottom lip.

Perfect. Just the woman I want to see.

She's so beautiful. I could just stare at her for hours. I could spend an entire day just watching the way the sunlight played in her hair and it would be a day well spent. I wish that I could go over and kiss her and tell her that I'm going to make everything right.

"I just wanted to check up on Rocky," she admits. "Is he alright? Audrey sent me over to give you some probiotics."

She produces an injection-like tube and Rocky's ears perk up.

"She said they're actually supposed to love them, despite the packaging," Ada smiles. "They have yeast or something in them. But anyways, I'm rambling now."

I take the probiotics from her hand with a smile and motion for her to sit down in the interview chair. She hesitates for a moment during which my heart almost stops. Ada glances back toward the café, but finally, she sits down next to Rocky and me. I can barely contain my smile.

I take a deep breath. I can do this. I can make things right between us. I have to make things better. I need her in my life and I don't want to lose her before we've even had a chance.

"I wanted to thank you again," I tell her. "I've been a total dick to you, Ada, and I'm well aware of it."

She's silent, but I can see the hint of a smile on the corner of her lips, and it urges me to go on.

"I was wondering if you'd join me - and Rocky, of course - for dinner tonight. My place," I say nervously, giving her a hopeful look.

Ada stares back at me and I'm worried she'll say no right away. But finally, she just shrugs.

"I won't be a pain," I promise her. "And I won't ignore you tomorrow. I'll be the man you deserve."

"Fine," Ada finally accepts. "But know that I'm mostly coming because of Rocky."

We both smile as she leans under the desk, scratching behind the dog's ears. Rocky barks appreciatively and Ada gets up.

"Should I bring something?" she asks me as an afterthought. "Dessert?"

"You can bring your friends if you'd like," I suggest.

She's surprised by my invitation, but she tries hard to hide it. I guess she thought it would only be the two of us, but I'm working hard to be a better man, and tonight, I'm going to show a vulnerable side of me to everyone.

"I'm inviting Sydney and Layla," I add. "Just let me have an idea for numbers. I'll make extra, but I'd hate to run out."

"Well, alright," Ada drawls. "I'll ask my friends if they want to come. But - your place? You sure you want to have that many people around?"

"I am," I reply. "It's all part of Nathaniel Rhodes version 2.0."

"I see," Ada grins at me. "Well, it seems like post-puppy Nate really is nicer."

She winks at me and heads back inside, and I sit there with a silly smile on my face for the next twenty minutes.

I leave Rocky with Layla while I go grocery shopping. She's thrilled to puppy-sit out on the front patio of Perk Me Up. She snuggles with the little guy, making sure he drinks water and regularly gets to go walk around. I couldn't ask for a better dog-aunt to make sure he's feeling better.

I go a little overboard at the grocery store. Everything has to be perfect, so I come up with every possible option. I make sure there is a vegetarian, vegan, and peanut-free option. I have no idea if any one of my guests is actually any of those things, but better safe than sorry. I want everyone to feel included tonight. My cart is so full I have trouble wheeling it to the cash register, and I have to call Layla to help me carry everything up.

We pile the groceries on the center island, food and ingredients piled high like treasure. Rocky wanders around the room before settling down in the center of my bed. I figure that I will never sleep alone now. He's claimed that bed as his too. I find that I don't actually mind.

"Did you know this is my first time in your apartment?" Layla puts her hands on her hips and looks around in an appreciative way that makes me feel good about the space. "I gotta say, though, I was expecting something more ominous. Maybe a red room?"

"Maybe I just don't show that to first-timers," I tell her. I frown. "Have you really never been up here?"

Layla shakes her head. "Nope. I've come up to the door to get you, but never been inside." She looks around again. "I'm surprised it's not just filled with pizza boxes and dirty clothes."

I roll my eyes at her. "That's what your house looks like."

"And it is the mark of a comfortable home," she assures me. She motions to all the food. "So, what are you making?"

I grin at her. "Everything."

"Mind if I hang out?" she asks, sitting down on my barstool.

Rocky paws at her leg, giving her sad puppy eyes, and she lifts him up into her lap, cooing at him. She presses her nose against his and he licks her.

"Sure," I tell her. "But you're not allowed to help."

"Wasn't going to." She grins. "I'm perfectly happy spending some quality time with Mr. Puppers over here."

I show her to the living room area, turn on Netflix for her, and then get to work.

It's time to be like my mother.

We're here. I text, my hand shaking slightly. I'm more nervous than I'd like to admit.

Come right on up. The reply is nearly immediate.

"Are you excited?" Audrey pokes my side, and I laugh, pushing her off.

"Shut up," I tell her, reaching into my bag for my camera. I snap a picture of her annoyed face and she rolls her eyes.

"She is," Jacob nods gravely. "You can tell by the way she's blushing. Usually when she's embarrassed, it's just her cheeks. But this time it's the neck as well."

"For crying out loud," I grumble, suddenly feeling incredibly self-conscious. Am I always this easy to read?

Jacob and Audrey exchange knowing looks and I

scowl at them, feeling the familiar heat creeping up my neck just like they said. My body is such a traitor.

I let us in through the back of Perk Me Up, and we walk the now-familiar path up the stairway to Nathaniel's place. The stairs creak slightly under the wait of the three of us, but remain solid. It's almost as if the house is excited to have this many guests.

The three of us stand awkwardly in front of Nate's front door, and I extend an arm to knock on the wood. Before I even have time to remove my hand, the door flies open and we're greeted by Layla, who has a big grin on her face.

"Hello, coffee lovers," she greets us, ushering us all in.

Rocky is all over us, so happy to have some more company. He wriggles and begs for all the pets, but still behaves himself. I take his picture several times making sure to catch his doggy smile.

"Wow," Audrey says, looking around. "This place is even better on the inside."

I have to agree. This place really is amazing. It's warm and homey. I'm glad he's finally letting more people come here - it would be a shame to hide it from his friends.

I guess that's what we are now - friends. *Just* friends.

Regret fills my mind, and I hold back a sigh. Sydney is sitting on the couch waiting for us. Layla sits next to her, the two of them pull Jacob and Audrey into a conversation about football. Since that isn't something I know much about, I decide to find Nate.

Soft rock music is playing in the background, and the place looks absolutely spotless. Something smells absolutely amazing and my stomach rumbles. I head over to the kitchen, leaving the others to fight over what to watch.

"Smells divine," I say, stepping into the kitchen. All the lights are on and it looks professional. There's even fresh flowers sitting on the counter. They look like something Layla picked out and I wish that I'd thought of that.

Nate turns around to face me, wearing a big grin and a cheesy apron that says Kiss the Chef. I wish I could kiss him, but then I remember how it had felt to wake up and find him gone.

"Thank you," he winks at me.

"I didn't know you were much of a cook," I add, sitting down on a bar stool at the counter. I pull out my camera and snap some shots of him cooking.

"Neither did I," he admits. "Here, try this."

He comes closer with a wooden spoon, filled with a red wine sauce. I look into his eyes as I taste it, and moan with pleasure.

"Good?" Nate asks hopefully.

"It's delicious," I admit.

"Awesome. I think it'll go great with the seafood, "Nate adds before turning back to the stove.

"Do you need any help?" I make sure to ask, even though I have a feeling he'll turn me down.

And he does exactly that, telling me to go hang out with everyone else while he prepares dinner. Hesitantly, I go back to the group, even though I'd rather stay on this stool.

Truth be told, I'm still a little angry. He claimed that he didn't call because his phone was broken, and maybe it was, but that still doesn't change how he's treated me. It didn't take away the heartache at calling and texting without response. I'd already decided to keep our relationship strictly professional - or a little friendly, maybe...

But now I'm thinking I might still want something more. The attraction between us is ever-present, and every time I'm near him, I crave Nathaniel Rhodes more and more. I just wish I knew that he felt that way too. I don't want to wake up and find him gone again.

"Dinner's served," Nate calls out to us about fifteen minutes later. He has all the food laid out on the kitchen counters, neatly displayed in glass bowls and serving trays. White wine is chilling in an ice bucket and he has a red wine breathing on the counter. The presentation looks better than some weddings I've been to.

There's everything from linguini with seafood, to a spinach salad with blue cheese and even a green bean casserole. I give Nate a curious look, wondering how he managed to prepare this feast in a matter of hours. For someone who doesn't know how to cook, he sure did a good job.

Honestly though, it shouldn't surprise me. He's a man of many talents and I know he can do practically anything if he decides he wants to.

The table is too small for all of us, since it was meant for two people, so Jacob and Layla settle at the counter instead, chattering about something or other. Sydney and Audrey claim the couch, so I'm left with a seat next to Nate at the table.

Before we start eating, Nate taps his fork against his wine glass. Our eyes all go to him, curious about what he has to say.

"Friends," he addresses us, awkwardly standing up and grinning at me as I take a sip of my white wine.

It's creamy and perfectly chilled. He really thought of everything.

"I wanted this evening to symbolize something new," Nate continues. "I wanted to make this a weekly thing. Call it "Dinners With Nate" or something. Truth is, you guys are the closest thing I have to... family."

He swallows hard, and I can tell he has trouble speaking. Without thinking, I gently squeeze his hand and he gives me a thankful look before starting up again.

"I've been pushing all of you away," he continues, looking at Layla first, and me second. "My friends. My coworkers. Even my regulars," he says, gesturing to Aubrey and Jacob. "I should have gotten to know you better all this time. Of course, I had my reasons. And at the time, I believed I was doing the right thing, but I now understand I was mistaken."

He sets his glass down.

"I hope you will all forgive me for my mistakes," he adds. "I hope we can move on and perhaps... become even better friends. Become a family. A dysfunctional, screwed-up family, but a family nonetheless."

We're all smiling now, and Audrey is even wiping a stray tear away.

Rocky ends the speech with an overly-excited bark and we all laugh before starting in on our food. Nate sits back down and I squeeze his hand again before he pulls away to pick up his fork.

We take a few bites. It's delicious as it looked and I have to tell myself to slow down and not snarf as much of it as I can into my face. I look over at Nate and see that he's barely had any of his food.

I reach under the table and gently squeeze his thigh.

He looks up into my eyes, giving me a grateful look. I smile at him and he starts to eat. We remain like that for the rest of the meal, and if anyone else notices our private moment of intimacy, they don't say a word.

After dinner, we all settle on the large couch with plates of rhubarb crumble and homemade vanilla bean ice cream.

"This is so good," Layla groans, shoving a spoon of food into her mouth.

"It really is perfect," Jacob agrees with a nod.

"All we need is some coffee to wash it down," I say with a laugh, and everyone agrees that's a wonderful idea.

So we all file down into the coffee shop area, sitting at the counter while Sydney and I whip up everyone's drug of choice. Meryiah greets us all into the store as we bring her a plate of food to enjoy while she works. She grins and thanks us, happy to be included.

"Is your boyfriend coming?" Jacob asks Audrey.

She scowls at him. "He had to work." Her tone is sharp and unhappy, making me think that there is more to it than that, but then she quickly changes the subject to the new ice cream place opening up on campus.

The evening is balmy and pleasant, so we leave the door to the café open. I wander around the shop, snapping pictures of my friends and capturing this moment of joy. We're all laughing and chatting the night away, and at some point, I surprise myself by realizing this is one of the best nights of my life.

It isn't until we're all sitting down with steaming cups that I notice Nate is quiet and pensive. I nudge him gently, and he looks up with those puppy eyes that can only be compared to Rocky's.

"Everything alright?" I enquire.

"Yeah." Nate's tone is rigid, and I wonder what it is that he's not telling me.

I really wish he'd open up to me. I think it's the only way to make our relationship - or whatever this dance we're doing is called - work.

"Hey," I say softly. "You can tell me anything, you know that, right?"

"I know." Nate sighs, running his fingers through his dark hair. "Alright, I'll tell you what's going on. In fact, I'll tell all of you."

He gets up with that, and everyone's eyes go to him once more as he stands up to speak.

"You're all not just my friends, but the people who make Perk Me Up the home it has become for all of us," Nathaniel says. "And I think it's time I made a confession."

My breath catches as I wait for him to go on. Nate takes a deep breath before speaking again.

"A few years ago, I had this idea of a coffee shop, somewhere for my friends to hang out, somewhere I could put my ideas of a business to fruition. Unfortunately, I got lost along the way. I became too business-minded, too involved in the running of it to care about the reason I started - connecting people, making friends. Finding love."

His eyes go to mine, and I feel a blush creeping up on my cheeks.

"I took out a loan all those years ago," Nate continues. "A big loan, so I could start the business. And boy, was business booming. I was certain I'd be able to repay it in a year, maybe even less."

He looks down, and I can tell how hard this is for him. And I feel so proud of him.

"I ran into some trouble around that time. A family member of mine got very... ill. The medical bills piled up, and I was the only one who could help. The only one who could afford to pay for everything," he explains.

I feel tears pricking my eyes, but I manage to keep them at bay - for the time being, at least.

"I'm still paying for all those bills," Nate continues. "And every day, they only pile up more. And now Perk Me Up is in trouble. The loan I took out is due and I don't have the money."

Layla stands up, tears on her face. "Why didn't you tell me?" she asks hoarsely.

Nate merely shakes his head, saying, "I couldn't bother you with it. You have too much of your own stuff going on."

A small silence envelops us before Nathaniel speaks again.

"I am hoping for a miracle here," he says. "I need nothing short of it. We need to find a way to make Perk Me Up more profitable, and I've no idea in hell how we're supposed to do that. But if we don't repay the loan in a month and a half..."

He lets the sentence hang in the air, and we all shift uncomfortably.

"We'll find a way," I hear Jacob saying.

"We can all work together," Audrey nods.

"We can make it work," Layla promises. She goes and hugs Nate the way I wish I could.

"I'll do whatever I can," I add.

Nate looks out at us, his eyes bright. His Adam's apple bobs and he manages a small smile.

"I'm..." he starts to speak but his voice cracks. "I'm honestly speechless. You're all incredible, offering help like that."

I walk over to him and give him a hug right along with Layla. Slowly, everybody else joins in as well until we're a mess of tangled hands and tears.

"Okay, whose hand is on my butt?" Jacob asks, and we all laugh, coming apart from our group hug.

"Hey, if you need money..." I tell him.

"Have you been holding out on me this whole time and are a secret billionaire?" he asks, obviously trying to lighten the mood.

"No. But... my family does have money." I swallow hard.

"I was under the impression that you aren't close with them," Nate says, all the joking gone from his voice. His eyes find mine and I stare into his dark depths, wanting to lose myself in him.

"For you..." My voice catches. "For you, I'd ask. I would ask for you."

"Oh, Ada." He hugs me, even though we're just friends. It's a friend's hug, I tell myself. "Thank you. I don't want you to do that, but thank you for the offer."

"I would do it for you," I whisper. I mean it too. I'd walk through fire for him, even if we can never be. I can't help the way I feel for him.

"No, Ada." He shakes his head and smiles at me. "Although it means the world to me. Thank you."

I smile, not really having any good words to say. Luckily, Layla calls to him and I can pretend to sip on my coffee and imagine that I didn't just offer up a part of my soul.

But, for Nate and Perk Me Up, it would be worth the shame of going to my parents.

If Perk Me Up goes under, we will all lose our jobs. And we will lose the place that means so much to each and every one of us.

I will do everything in my power to help out Perk Me Up. And I will give Nate a second chance, because today, he showed me another part of himself. A part that is vulnerable, scared and small.

But a part that is beautiful nonetheless.

$\mathcal{N}$ ate

After my big confession, I feel as though a huge weight has fallen off my shoulders. I feel better. So much better I can hardly believe it, and seeing Ada in my apartment only makes my heart soar further. I like having her close. I like it when she's near me.

We stay at Perk Me Up until closing time and help Meryiah close everything down. She heads home to be with her family, but the rest of us take the party back upstairs.

We spend the rest of the evening laughing, eating more dessert and playing a board game I didn't even know I had. Rocky is completely worn out by the end of the night, and when Layla and Beccky announce they have to leave, he's already fast asleep in his doggy bed.

It's well past midnight when Audrey and Jacob collect

their things to go home. I look at Ada trying to decipher her mood. I can't tell whether she wants to leave with her friends or stay a little while longer alone with me. Well, with Rocky as a chaperone.

Ada and Audrey speak in hushed tones by the doorway. I pretend to do the dishes, but my ears strain to hear what she has decided to do. Will she stay or will she go?

And then Ada reappears in the kitchen and it's like a ray of sunshine just shone into my life, even though it's the middle of the night.

"Hey," she says easily, and a smile lights up her face.

"Hey," I reply, suddenly feeling a little unsteady on my feet. How is she so beautiful? She doesn't even mean to be, she just is. She is beautiful in every way from her smile to her disposition.

"I thought I'd stay for a while longer," Ada explains, shifting her weight from one foot to another. She plays with the silver charm on her necklace. "I thought I could help you out with the dishes or something. Is that alright?"

"Yeah," I say softly. "It's perfect."

We head into the kitchen and I put the music on louder while we clean up the mess. There's plates and glasses everywhere, but it's easy enough to clean up my home.

Ada chatters about her new classes, telling me how much she's enjoying them.

"I didn't know how much I'd like making videos," she tells me, stacking plates in a precarious pile to carry to the sink. "But it's all the things I like about photos, only more. I'm actually really excited for some of the projects we have to do."

I nod and ask questions, just enjoying her company. Doing the normal, boring parts of life feels like a pleasure with her. I don't have my chores when she does them with me. They feel like something I want to do with her to help.

When the dishwasher is running and the tables all cleaned, we plop down on the couch and high five each other for a job well done.

"Thank you," Ada says quietly. She sits next to me, close enough that we could touch, but still enough distance to maintain a semblance of propriety. "Thank you for inviting Jacob and Audrey tonight. They had a blast."

"What about you?" I ask. My heart is suddenly pounding in my chest. I want so badly to lean over and kiss her, but that would violate our friendship pact. I don't dare ruin that. "Did you have fun, too?"

Ada looks right into my eyes, and breaks into a smile. "Yeah. I definitely did. I'm really glad I came."

Relief I didn't know I needed washes through me. It's like cool water on a hot day, refreshing and wonderful. I didn't know how nervous I'd been for tonight to go well until Ada told me it was a success.

"Hey, mind if I make some more dessert?" Ada asks me.

"Not at all," I reply. "We have some leftover ice cream, but we're out of the crumble."

"That's actually perfect." Ada's eyes sparkle with mischief.

"What are you planning?" I ask her as she gets up from the couch, practically dancing her way into the kitchen.

"Just you wait and see," she grins back, and I follow

closely behind as she starts pulling a pan out from under the oven. "Where do you keep the sugar?" Ada asks, peering into one of my cupboards.

"Right in front of me." I motion to her whole body and wink. Ada rolls her eyes, but she grins at me.

"I asked for sugar, not cheese." She sticks her tongue out at me, putting one hand on a hip.

"Alright, alright." I raise my hands up in defeat. "Second cupboard to the left. What do you need it for anyway?"

"I'm making something to go with the ice cream," Ada tells me mysteriously.

She gathers a couple other ingredients from my pantry, and I sit down on the counter, watching her work her magic.

She puts a small saucepan on the stove, and starts melting sugar with honey and a little bit of lemon juice.

I watch with wonder as the sauce starts bubbling and a delicious scent envelops us. Even Rocky raises his head and gives the air a tentative whiff.

Ada grabs two bowls, filling them with the plain vanilla ice cream. With a gin in my direction, she pours the hot sauce over the ice cream, creating a gooey delicious coating that I can't wait to try.

She hands me one of the bowls and waits for me to try it. I take a small bite, finding the cold of the ice cream is decadent against the heat of the caramel.

"Oh god," I say, taking a giant bite this time and stuffing it in my mouth with pleasure. "What is this? It's so fucking good."

"Some Jones family-style caramel," Ada replies with a

wink, but she seems a little solemn as we finish our midnight snack.

"You don't talk about your parents much," I realize out loud.

"Neither do you." She winks at me, throwing the ball back at me.

I can't help but laugh, saying, "Fair enough. A story for another day, perhaps."

She pauses. "My dad used to make it when I was a kid. It was something just for the two of us. My mom thought sugar would make me fat, so he didn't make it very often."

I chew on the delicious caramel, absorbing her words.

"My dad never cooked. My mom did," I tell her. "She loved dinner parties. I think she would have liked me throwing this one. I think she made sure I didn't burn any of it."

"She would have been proud of you," she tells me, her eyes solemn and big as she looks at me.

"Thanks," I tell her. "I think I channeled her a little bit tonight."

"I love that we're talking again," Ada remarks a moment later. She stares into her empty bowl, fiddling with the spoon. She's not smiling. "But there is something I need to tell you. It's kind of important."

My heart stalls. This is where she tells me she found someone else. Or that she doesn't want a commitment right now. Or that she's moving to Greece.

"You've got caramel sauce all over your cheek." She grins at me and I breathe out in relief.

"Where?" I ask with mock shock, clutching my heart.

"All over," Ada laughs.

I lick the side of my mouth. "Better?"

"You only made it worse. Come over here."

I scoot closer obediently and Ada wipes some caramel off my cheek. Suddenly, the whole room feels like it's been charged with electricity. We're staring at each other, and we both want this. Want each other.

I let her take the lead. Ada leans in closer and kisses me. Her tongue is tart and sweet, absolutely delicious.

"I want you," she says against my lips, and it sends shivers down my spine.

"Are you sure?" I ask softly.

I don't want her to regret this. I've been a prick to her before, and now it's time for Ada to call the shots. If she tells me she'd rather be just friends, I'm ready to respect her decision.

I can see the internal battle going on inside her head. She puts her hands on my chest, not pushing me away, but not pulling me closer as she decides what she wants. Finally, she kisses me again, and my heart soars.

"I'm sure," she whispers.

I don't need to be told twice.

*N*ate

We look at each other for a long time and finally, I take the plunge and lean down until my lips touch Ada's. She grabs the back of my neck and pulls me down into a full-blown kiss, her tongue exploring my mouth.

She moans against me and I groan right back. She smells like cinnamon and sugar, all sweetness and spice. I inhale her scent, breathing her into my own body and making her a part of me.

"I missed you," Ada murmurs against my mouth.

"I missed you more," I tell her, biting on her lower lip gently.

We kiss differently than we did before now. Like we know a little bit more about each other. And like we're excited to find out every bit that makes us who we are.

Our make out session is cut short when Rocky bites on my pants, growling and almost pulling them off me. Laughing, I climb off Ada and pet the dog.

"See, he's got the right idea," Ada winks at me.

"Oh yeah?" I cock my head to the side. "You gonna take my pants off next?"

"I just might." She winks at me, gets up from the couch and stretches.

Her tee rides up and I'm left staring dumbfounded at the sliver of naked skin it exposes. I can feel the blood rush south and I strain against the fabric of my pants. Ada's eyes glance at my crotch and she grins, stretching up just a bit more, giving me a show.

"I think it's just past his bedtime," I say, giving the dog a glare. He cocks his head, floppy ears innocent. "Because you wouldn't cock block me, would you, Rocky?"

"Maybe he thought he was protecting me," Ada says, lowering her arms. She grins, a devilish look that has my blood pumping. "You were about to ravish me."

I look back at the dog. "You don't need to protect her."

Rocky doesn't do anything but wag his tail at me. I sigh and go to the kitchen. Rocky's tail wags harder, banging on the floor.

I give him one of the red rubber treat balls stuffed with peanut butter the vet recommended. Rocky happily takes it in his mouth and settles on his blanket by the fire. He chews on it for a moment before giving me a look that says, "What? Go do what you were going to do. I'm happy now."

"So, about those pants..." Ada is suddenly beside me, her hands on my waistband. She looks up at me, her lower lip caught between her teeth and eyes wide and anything but innocent.

I reach for her, wrapping my hands around the back of her neck and tangling in her soft hair to bring her in for another kiss. The scent of coffee and cinnamon fills the air and I think it's the best scent I've ever smelled.

"Maybe the bedroom this time?" she asks, glancing toward the laundry room and then back at me.

I chuckle, sliding my hands under her shirt, feeling the soft skin at her hips and stomach. "If I can keep my hands off you long enough to get there."

She flashes me a grin and darts into the bedroom. She giggles, playfully as I chase after her, hot on her tail.

I love the way she laughs, vibrant and youthful as she sprints into the bedroom, shrieking with delight as I grab for her. She skitters just out of my grasp, falling onto the bed.

"That won't save you," I growl, lunging onto the bed and pinning her there. She struggles, but not hard enough to tell me she wants to escape. I take both her wrists in one hand, pinning them over her head.

She could easily pull free if she wanted to, but instead she writhes under me, undulating her hips to grind against me. I kiss her, nipping at her bottom lip and keeping her pinned. With my free hand I trace the line from her wrists, down her arms, and tease the small sliver of skin at her abdomen not hidden by her shirt.

She whimpers, arching her hips. I slide my hand under her shirt, feeling the soft skin of her belly and working upward. Her bra is lacey beneath my fingers as I cup her breast for a moment. I slide my hand back down to the button of her jeans.

Years of practice has her pants button undone. I pull down on the zipper, my breath catching at the sinfully lacey panties that peek out of the fabric. My eyes go to hers.

"What?" she asks innocently. "A girl can't look pretty?"

I let go of her wrists, but she keeps her arms up. I tug on her pants and she lifts her hips, slithering out of the denim. My mouth waters at the sight of her.

Long beautiful legs that lead to delicate lacey panties in a pale blue that accentuate the curve of her perfect hips. She's flawless. Her blue and white striped shirt is still high enough to show off her bellybutton.

I take the hem of her shirt and she sits up to let me lift it over her head.

She lays back on the pillows of my bed, her arms still up and over her head as if I still held her.

She is a goddess. She is all sweet curves and feminine beauty that makes me want to cream my pants just looking at her. She looks like something out of a Playboy Magazine, something that I should lust and idolize, but never actually have the chance to have.

"I think you have too many clothes on," she tells me. Her voice is husky and her eyes are dark with desire.

I unbutton my shirt, carelessly tossing it to the floor behind me. She rubs one long leg against the other, squirming in those delicate panties that I can't seem to stop staring at.

"More," she commands.

I remove my pants, my briefs, and socks as quickly as I can. I stand before her at the foot of the bed, staring up at my goddess.

She smiles, looking me up and down. "That's better," she purrs.

"Keep your hands up," I tell her, placing one hand on each of her ankles. She looks confident and sexy as I slide my hands up her legs, feeling the smooth skin of her calves, her thighs and then the lace.

I let my fingers trace the delicate flowers embroidered in the lace right above the spot that I know causes her the most pleasure. She whimpers, arching her hips into my touch. She's already dripping with excitement and my own cock starts to ache to fill her.

I hook my fingers over the waistband of the panties and slowly pull them down. I take my time, not hurrying, not rushing. Our first time was all need and lust, lost in our own passions. I didn't give her the pleasure she deserved.

I plan on fixing that tonight.

Slowly, I lower my mouth to the apex of her thighs. She goes statue still, but lets me spread her legs wide enough for me to kneel comfortably at her altar.

And there I worship her. I use my tongue and lips to suck and tickle. My fingers slide into the sweet wetness of her, my own cock jealous of my hands as I pump pleasure into her. Her fingers tangle in my hair as she directs me as to what will give her the most pleasure.

I live for the little groans and gasps as I find the motions that make her body writhe. She tastes like caramel to my tongue, sweet and rich, as I taste and feast on her. Her hips start to shake, her thighs begin to tremble.

"Nate…"

I love the way she gasps my name. I plan on having her scream it in a moment.

Her back arches, her eyes closing and mouth going wide. I smile, keeping the rhythm of my fingers and tongue steady as she climaxes beneath me. She so sweet and delicious, I wish I could simply feast on her for the remainder of the night.

But my cock wants more. Needs more.

She lays gaspsing on the bed, her eyes glassy and expression far away. I go to the nightstand and pull out a condom. I slide it on and I'm back over her in time to see her smile at me.

"Your turn," she says. Her voice has the husky pleasure of sex in it as she grabs my hips and guides me into her waiting warmth.

God, she feels so good. She's so tight and wet that my eyes involuntarily roll back into my head and every thought disappears. She is everything I could ever want. Everything I could ever need.

I once again pin her hands over her head. She writhes in time with my thrusts, not fighting my control, but letting me find pleasure in her body. She increases the pleasure, using her own hips and muscles to milk and squeeze my cock.

It's heaven. Pure and simple. She is an angel with her hair spread out on the pillow like a halo and her skin gleaming in the pale light. Her breasts bounce in the beautiful lace of her bra, threatening to spill out but staying put.

Every thrust makes it harder to think. Her body feels so damn good that I can't stop. I won't stop.

And then she cries out my name. Her back arches, her

eyes rolling back in her head and her breasts jutting up to the sky. Her hands press against my hold on her, her hips beginning to shake like they did when I was tasting her.

I feel her orgasm around me. I feel the pleasure wash through her, the way she tightens and squeezes, her hips spasming and bucking.

And it feels so damn good that I lose myself in her. I let go. I let go of all my worries and let her pleasure take me over the edge into my own heaven. She is my heaven. She is everything I could ever want, everything I could ever need.

I lower my head, kissing her. She kisses me back, panting and smiling.

"You are amazing," she gasps, finally wiggling free of my grip so she can pull my head into a deeper kiss. I let her escape, wanting her to kiss me more than I want the illusion of control.

"No, you," I reply, nuzzling the curve of her shoulder, and letting my weight settle on her for a moment. She sighs with contentment, wrapping her arms around my shoulders and her legs around mine so I can't escape.

Not that I want to. I could stay here like this forever and die a happy man.

But time is always moving forward. There is no way to stay in a moment.

She kisses me and yawns, making me yawn as well. I remember just how late it is and that we both have to work tomorrow.

Only then do I pull out of her, discard of the condom in my bedroom bin, and crawl back between the sheets with Ada by my side. She feels so good next to me, filling a hole in my bed that had always seemed empty without her.

I let Ada pull me closer and I hug her back. We don't say anything after that - we don't need to. We both know we just connected more deeply and ever.

I don't know when I fall asleep, but when I do, my wonderful dreams are filled with Ada.

Always Ada.

 da

I wake up with a start. Not because I'm in Nathaniel's bed - no, I'm damn pleased about that, to say the least. He made me come better than I ever have before last night, and I'm going to make him do it again and again in the future.

No, I have an idea. I can't believe I didn't think of it before. It should have been obvious to me, but as I'm learning in my social media classes, just because it's obvious doesn't mean it won't work. Sometimes those are the best ways to get customers.

I look at Nate. He looks softer in his sleep, younger and less worried. Sometimes I forget how different our ages are. I forget that he's older than I am, but that doesn't mean that I can't help him. I want to help him. I want to take all his cares and make him feel as wonderful as he makes me feel.

Rocky is curled up against his shoulder. He's outgrown the first collar Nate got him, and the current one is looking like it won't fit for long. Pretty soon that little fluffy ball of caramel colored fur is going to take up the entire bed. The dog snores, but he's obviously, thoroughly, in love with Nate. I can't blame Rocky.

I think I might be a little in love with him too.

I close the bedroom door behind me, and head into Nate's kitchen. It doesn't take me long to find all the things I need and figure out how to work his fancy little espresso machine and milk foamer.

I put on an apron and get to work.

In twenty minutes' time, the kitchen is filled with steam and coffee cups litter the counters. I'm stirring something on the stove, feeling every bit the mad scientist I am. Everything I've made has been delicious, but they all seem to be missing something.

I glance around the counter. Cinnamon? Cardamom? Ginger? More sugar?

My eyes settle on a fancy bottle of pink himalayan rock salt.

Something inside of me clicks and I grin, bringing the salt over to my concoction station.

I foam up some more milk and pour myself another cup of coffee, just as I hear footsteps approaching me. I look up distracted, but my face transforms from a scowl into a smile when I see Nate approaching me.

"Good morning, Newbie," Nate drawls out. Something deep in my chest warms at the nickname.

"Hey," I reply.

"What have you been up to?" he reaches for one of my first attempts at this recipe. I snatch the cup away from him and dump it in the sink.

Nate stares at the coffee draining down the sink, giving me an amused look.

"Everything alright, gorgeous?" he asks me, sounding almost worried, but I reassure him with a big smile.

"Everything's great," I tell him. "In fact, better than great. But I need you to do me a favor."

"Okay," Nate replies doubtfully.

"Taste this." I present him with another cup of coffee - my sixth of the day, in fact - and Nate takes it from me, giving it a long whiff.

"Smells great," he remarks with a smile.

"I hope it tastes great too." I bite my lip as I wait for him to taste it. "I've been trying recipes for a while now, but I think this one might be a winner. Try it, please."

I watch Nate eagerly as he takes his first sip of coffee, and slowly swallows the warm liquid. The tension is killing me, and I need to know whether he likes it or not.

"Well?" I ask expectantly. I'm bouncing on the balls of my feet and have way too much caffeine in my system.

"It's..." He's teasing me, and we both know it, but I can't grinning back at him.

"It's really good, Ada," he finally admits, rolling his tongue around his mouth to - I hope - savor the taste."What is it?"

"Caramel," I explain with a smile, finally lowering down off my toes and settling on the ground again.

"Like the one you made yesterday," Nate realizes. I nod.

"Like the one you were trying to make," I add.

"Only… it's actually edible." Nate is laughing, shaking his head. He takes another sip. "This is really delicious, Newbie. Is there something else in there?"

"It's salted caramel," I explain. "I thought it would go well with the coffee flavor."

"It really does," Nate replies. "It tastes amazing. Would you be okay if I offer this in the shop?"

"Yeah," I reply with a big grin. "Definitely. That's why I came up with it."

"Wait, you did this for me?" he asks, his eyes going wide. He looks down at the coffee like I just handed him a million dollars.

"Yeah." I shrug and give him a shy grin.

He puts down his coffee cup and pulls me in for a hug. I only notice then that he is still wearing just boxers, and my body melts into him. He smells like pine and coffee again. And salted caramel. I really want him. Really really want him.

"Should we…" I say, my voice hoarse.

"Get back to bed?" Nate finishes my sentence, and I smile guiltily.

"I think we should, yes," he replies.

He smacks my ass and I follow him out of the kitchen. At the bedroom door, Nate raises a finger in the air as if he's forgotten something, heads back into the kitchen and reappears a moment later with the coffee cup I gave him.

"I want to finish this," he explains guiltily, and it makes me grin wider than ever.

He really does like my new flavor then. Today couldn't have started in a better way.

～

Nate and I spend another hour in bed, until I'm so horrendously late for my shift I feel my cheeks burning up, knowing Sydney is handling the lunch crowd without me. I finally manage to convince Nate to let me go, even though he is a grumpy bastard about it.

I wear yesterday's clothes, and rush into the coffee shop area to find Sydney flustered, but smiling wide.

"Long night?" she asks me, bumping her hip into mine. She grins at me. "That's a good look on you."

"Thanks," I reply, grateful for her kindness.

We work together in quiet companionship, and the clock ticks by. Meryiah comes and replaces Sydney and we talk about how good Nate's cooking was last night. Finally, near the end of my shift, Nate pokes his head through the kitchen and motions for me to follow him. I'm about to clock out anyway, so I take my apron off and head into the kitchen

In the kitchen, I'm greeted by Nate and Layla. I grin when I see her, and she pulls me in for a friendly hug.

"Hey, girl," she says with a big smile.

"Hey," I reply with a matching smile for her. "What are you doing here? I thought your shift wasn't for a few days."

"We have a little surprise for you," Nate tells me with a sly grin, and I give him a surprised look.

They both step aside, revealing a chalkboard we usually place in front of the coffee shop. Today, it's been revamped from the usual "Croissant and latte, special price!" and is wearing a new design.

Salted Caramel is written on the board, decorated with a pretty drawing of fallen leaves. Whoever wrote it is great at calligraphy as the writing is truly beautiful - an accomplishment, since it's done in chalk.

"Wow," I say right away, unable to wear the big smile that dominates my face.

"You like it?" Layla asks anxiously.

"It's amazing." I nod with enthusiasm. "You did this?"

She shrugs shyly and I compliment her again. She really is a talented artist, and I love the way she brought the new flavor to life. The colors truly capture the feeling of autumn, which is what I wanted this drink to taste like. I turn to face Nate next.

"So you're really doing this?" I ask him. "You're going to launch this as your new flavor?"

He nods. "If you're sure you're alright with it, of course."

"More than alright," I admit with a big smile. "I'm actually honored."

"Happy to hear that," Nate tells me, putting his hand on my shoulder. It's a friendly gesture, but we exchange a heated glance, both knowing we want to touch in a much friendlier version, but not with Layla around. Her wicked little grin tells me she knows exactly what's going on between the two of us.

"We'll officially launch the flavor in two days," Nate tells me. "But I need you to teach everyone how to make it before then."

I reach for my necklace, feeling the comforting slide of the charm along the silver chain. "Would it be okay to post some things on social media about this?" I ask. "I have homework due in my media classes and this would actually really help my grade."

"You get a good grade and the shop gets publicity," Layla answers for Nate. "I say it's a win all around."

Nate laughs. "I'm just glad I have someone who actually likes all this technology. It's beyond me."

"You old fogey," Layla teases. "It's a good thing you got yourself a spring chicken."

"It helps that he's cute," I tell her.

Layla laughs. "I'll go grab the staff that's here and you can teach us the recipe."

I wait until Layla is out of earshot.

"It also helps that you have an amazing cock," I whisper to Nate.

He laughs in a way that drops the years, pulling me to him in a hug that has me heating in all the right places. I very much don't want to make caramel. I want to make love upstairs.

However, I know how much this cafe means to Nate. To me. To all my friends.

To my new family.

And suddenly, making caramel coffee is all I want to do,because for the first time in a very long while, I feel like I have a family.

I feel like I belong.

I hope I can do this. I hope I can save the coffee shop, and not have anything else come in and mess this up for us.

ate

The salted caramel coffee is a hit.

I knew it would be. The moment I tasted Ada's creation, I knew that it was the thing that could vault us into Best Coffee Shop this year. Already the news is spreading and we're selling more caramel coffee lattes than anything else.

I don't dare breathe a sigh of relief yet though, but it is nice to have something that feels like it's going right for a change.

On day four of the launch, I wake up disappointed to find that Ada isn't in my bed. She had a test today, so she slept at her own house. I now find that I don't like to sleep alone.

Well, I'm not truly alone. Rocky is turning into a terrible bed hog.

I head downstairs and work in my office for a little while, watching the clock. Ada's shift starts at one. I tell myself that I will just work until then, but I get hungry and head out to the kitchen to grab a muffin.

And find Ada prepping a giant batch of her caramel.

"What are you doing here?" I ask her. I'm not even mad that she didn't come say hello. I'm just glad to see her. "I thought you had a test."

"I did. It went fine." She grins at me. "I'm here because you're going to need all the help you can get today. I came in early."

I frown. "What do you mean?" Sydney hasn't called for help, but then Layla has a way of showing up when I don't notice. I've been busy in the office paying bills and working on payroll. No one seems to want to bother me when I'm doing payroll. They all want to get paid.

Ada finishes the caramel and pulls out her phone. She hands it to me and a video starts to play on screen. I recognize the song as one of the more popular ones that plays here.

Fall leaves swirl across the campus, their golden edges bright in the late afternoon light. The image shifts to the cafe with a closeup of our new salted caramel coffee being made by hand. Friends all sit out in the sunshine laughing and sipping on the coffee.

"It's a nice video," I comment, handing the phone back to Ada. "Did you make it?"

"Yup." She grins. "It went viral. It has over a million views on TikTok and nearly that many on Instagram."

"Is that good?" I'm not sure that something going viral is a good thing. Colds are viral.

"It's amazingly good," Ada assures me. "When I was on

campus, I heard at least three different people talking about it today."

"Hey, are you done with that caramel?" Sydney interrupts, poking her head into the kitchen. "I'm out and need more."

"Already?" Ada asks. She hands Sydney the batch she just finished. "I'll get another ready."

"Thanks." Sydney looks at me. "Can you see if Meryiah can come in early? I've got orders out the door. Layla and I are slammed."

I blink slowly at her as she disappears back to the front of the cafe.

Orders out the door.

"Told you it was going to be a busy day," Ada says, starting a new batch of caramel on the stove.

A full week of non-stop customers.

And then another.

I'm going to have to hire another barista, although I have a feeling the new person will never be as good as Ada.

This month I am able to pay the loan shark payment off before the reminders come. It's an amazing feeling to finally feel like I might be getting ahead.

I will need this stream of customers to keep up, but for the first time in months, I feel like I might be able to pay off the loan.

I let myself feel happy.

I'm almost giddy with excitement, and it's not a feeling I'm very familiar with. I'm usually always worried, always on the lookout for the nearest sight of trouble that could mean an end to our business. But not this time. This time, I'm letting myself be optimistic.

Ada assures me that she will keep the videos going. It feels like she has a new viral video every day, although she assures me that it's not that amazing. It feels amazing to me.

I can't remember the last time I had to make a double inventory order. The bakery across the street can hardly keep up with our new need of caramel scones and apple fritters.

It's a good problem to have.

"I'm just going to hop in the shower real quick," Ada tells me after a late afternoon walk with Rocky after a busy morning of making caramel. "Then we should go grab some dinner."

"How about that sushi place?" I offer. She more than deserves the treat.

Ada grins at me. "I'll be quick."

I hear the water turn on and consider hopping in with her, except we won't end up showering. We'll end up just getting sweatier and stickier, which isn't a bad thing, except that I'm hungry.

I sit on the couch and Rocky hops up beside me, curling up in a warm ball of sandy fur, his head on my lap. His brown eyes are watching the bathroom door though. Sometimes I think he loves Ada more than me.

I can't say that I blame him. The dog has good taste.

I also enjoy that Ada now keeps a stash of clothes here. It has made the late nights working so much better, even though it usually means we're both late to work or school in the morning.

I pet Rocky's head and he closes his eyes, sighing with contentment. I sigh with him. His ears are velvet soft and his fur is coming in. The vet seems to think that he's part poodle and that he won't shed much. I certainly haven't noticed any fur on my couch, which I appreciate. His caramel colored fur is curly but soft and I hope that he keeps the teddy-bear look he has going.

The water turns off in the bathroom. I slide out from under Rocky, the puppy whining slightly when I leave, but staying on the couch. He'll get up when Ada comes out.

The phone rings in my pocket. This time I'm not afraid that it's the loan coming due. It's probably just the cafe telling me that we're running low on sugar packets again.

Except it's not. A cold sweat breaks out as I see the caller ID.

Brookdale Assisted Living and Memory Care.

My heart stalls and I feel like my knees are going to give out. I can barely press the green phone to answer.

"This is Nathaniel Rhodes," I say with a shaky voice.

"Mr. Rhodes?" the voice on the other side of the line asks. "There's been a problem here. It concerns your father."

*N*ate

My whole body shakes and I crumple into the couch with a soft thud. Rocky seems to sense my worry, gently nudging me in the foot with his snout. Ada chooses that exact moment to walk out of the bathroom, body still wet from her shower.

I feel numb. I listen to the woman on the other line and my whole body convulses, threatening to break out in sobs. All the good feelings from earlier are gone like water down the drain.

"So I've been thinking," Ada is saying. "How do you feel about a salted caramel brownie?"

She's wearing a huge grin on her face as she turns to face me, but it disappears as soon as she sees the state I'm in.

Ada walks over to me, reaching me faster than I

thought she would. Her hands wrap around me and she gently pries the telephone from my hands.

"Hello, this is Ada Jones speaking," she says softly into it, her hand coming to rest on my shoulder. "Mr. Rhodes needs a moment."

She listens to what the woman on the other line is saying, nodding slowly. Once they are finished, she nods and thanks her for calling. Then, she disconnects the call and places the telephone on the coffee table in front of us.

She kneels down before me, her hands on my knees. She's looking into my eyes, but my own are floating away. I feel a thousand miles away from my apartment. I feel completely and utterly lost.

"Do you know where we need to go?" Ada asks me calmly, and I nod on auto-pilot. "Okay. Let's put on some clean clothes and go," Ada says as if it really is as simple as that.

We both get up and she helps me get into a pair of trousers and a shirt. She buttons it up for me and helps me put on a blazer. She dresses herself next, wearing a simple pair of dark wash jeans and a burgundy, soft cotton tee that looks amazing on her. I'm noticing anything and everything but what's important, my eyes focusing on our clothes and my mind gripping onto the materials and colors. Anything to help me forget about what's really going on.

Ada finds my car keys and asks me if I know the address. I nod, but I can't even speak. She hands me a pad of paper and a pen, and with shaky hands, I scribble down the name of where we need to be. She pulls up the directions on the GPS.

"Alright, it's gonna be alright," Ada keeps telling me, but I have trouble believing her.

I've had panic attacks before, but this isn't something I'm used to. I feel so pathetic, like I can't do a single thing - not even breathe. My throat is closed up and I can't inhale. I feel like my chest is going to burst open, or my body will just catch on the fire from the heat that envelops me.

Instead, nothing happens. Apart from the war that rages in my mind, I seem to be alright. I follow Ada downstairs, and she quickly asks Sydney to check on Rocky when her shift ends. Sydney promises to take him all afternoon and I'm grateful.

Ada steers me to the shared garage space the buildings on the street share. I have an older model Audi that chirps as Ada unlocks the doors. I'm glad she's happy to drive because I am not in a good state at the moment.

It feels like my world is crashing down. A slow collapse, like watching a river sweep away a house. It's slow, but unstoppable and horrifying to watch.

It's about a one hour drive. Ada turns on the radio, choosing a classical music radio station. I know she's trying to find something calming, but my mind is focusing on the last puzzle piece that makes me the man I am today. The one piece Ada still has to fit into the whole picture.

My father.

Ada holds my hand the whole ride. She doesn't let me go or ask me to explain. She is just there for me.

Absent-mindedly, I make a note to myself to repay her somehow once we get home. Somehow, that mental note makes me feel better. It tells me there will be an after, and I will be okay. I will get through this. I can make plans for later today, so surely, I will live through the next few hours.

We leave our small town and fly down the highway past fields of corn and wheat. Slowly, the crops turn into business and homes as we approach the outskirts of the city. Ada takes an exit off the highway, following a large road to a medical facility.

Brookdale Assisted Living and Memory Care, the plaque on the lawn reads. The name sounds nice, but I hate it here. I hate what this place represents. I hate every time I come here and see how far he's fallen.

"Ada," I struggle to say. My feet don't seem to want to walk into the main entrance.

She stops, pulling on my hand slightly. She walks back to me and cups my face in her hands, kissing my lips ever so softly.

"You don't need to tell me," she says simply.

"I know," I admit brokenly. "But I want to."

She squeezes my hand reassuringly, and I take a deep breath before continuing to speak.

"My father, he…" The lump in my throat is enormous, and I'm having trouble breathing.

"It's okay," Ada tells me, seeing how hard talking about this is for me. "I understand. I'll keep my distance, but I'm here if you need me. You know that, right, Nathaniel?"

I nod, offering her a weak smile. I do know she is here for me. She's proven to be trustworthy, and right now, she is the most important person in my life.

"I'm glad you're here," I tell her honestly.

We link hands as we walk into the building. The first set of doors reminds me of a nice hotel. A woman in scrubs is waiting at the front desk to greet us. We sign our names on a small sheet of paper and the woman brings us to another set of doors.

These ones are not glass and are not like a nice hotel. These are medical doors. We have to be buzzed in.

I hate this set of doors. I don't go past them if I can help it. I try to stay in the outside rooms where I can always escape.

The smell of bleach and old people floats in the air. It can't be helped in a place like this, but I still hate it. At least there are large windows letting in lots of light and comfortable chairs all over this particular lobby.

A nurse comes to greet us. She's wearing dark purple scrubs that make the silver in her hair shine and a friendly smile. I recognize her as one of the nurses that is often with my father. I think her name is Gail, but I'm here so infrequently that I'm not sure.

Guilt at that thought hits me. I am a terrible son.

"How is he?" I ask lamely.

"He'll be just fine," the nurse says with a firm smile. "We're not sure how he got out, but we managed to find him before the authorities needed to be called. He scraped up his hands pretty good, but no major injuries."

She turns to Ada. "And who is this lovely young lady?" she asks curiously.

I'll bet she wants to know. I've never come here with anyone, not even when I was dating Katy. She always said it was too depressing to come here with me, and the one time she drove me to the facility, she insisted on waiting in the parking lot.

"This is Ada Jones," I tell her.

"I believe we spoke on the phone," Ada says pleasantly, shaking her hand.

"Indeed we did," the nurse smiles at her.

"She's my girlfriend," I blurt out, surprising all three of us.

I can feel Ada's eyes on me, and I look at the floor nervously. I hope it doesn't bother her that I described her like that.

"It's so nice that you could come," Gail tells her. "Mr. Rhodes doesn't get many visitors. It's so nice to meet you."

Gail leads us down the hallway which is still terribly familiar, even though it's been months since the last time I came here. We stop in front of a room a few doors down, and I look through the small glass window on it, seeing a shape in a bed, covered by blankets. The TV is on, the blue light flickering against the closed curtains.

"You're free to go on," Gail tells me softly. "He's having a very rough day today."

"Alright." I swallow hard, looking at Ada for comfort.

She takes my hand, giving me a reassuring squeeze and a smile.

"I'll be right outside if there's anything you need," Gail tells me kindly, and I nod, knowing the whole routine by heart now.

I slowly open the door leading into my father's prison.

 ate

Ada and I head inside, and I almost feel my heartbeat in my throat. It's jumpy and irregular, and I feel faint again. But I manage to find the anxiety off, just like I always do when I'm with my father.

I walk a little in front of Ada. She walks slowly behind me, and we stop once we've reached my father's bed. My eyes linger on his figure, and I marvel at his small size.

The man was once enormous, a slab of muscle and a wall of determination. Today, he is not much more than a skeleton of his former self, a bag of bones and saggy skin. His graying hair is almost gone with only several tufts of puffy locks remaining. His eyes are hollow and a murky brown.

"Hello, Dad," I say softly, trying to hold back my tears.

He looks at me blankly, and my heart swells with hurt.

It really must be a bad day then. And he looks so very much worse than the last time I visited.

I sit down on the chair in front of the bed, and Ada stands by my side. She puts her hand on my shoulder and I draw strength from her touch.

"Dad, I heard something bad happened today," I tell my father. "They tell me you got lost outside."

Ada squeezes my shoulder, but my Dad merely stares at me. I notice that there are bandaids on his hands. I wonder how many times he fell before the nurses found him.

"You shouldn't do that," I say softly. "It's not good, Dad. What would I do if something happened to you?"

"You're doing just fine," Dad surprises me by replying. He even looks away from the TV.

I'm thrilled by the fact he's acknowledged me. This is how it is with Alzheimer's - sometimes he'll have a lucid moment amidst a sea of forgotten ones. Sometimes he'll be completely passive, other times he'll smile like he hasn't seen me in years.

I suppose he hasn't.

The last few times I visited, he made no sign of remembering who I was.

"I am doing fine," I reply with a smile, not hiding how pleased I am about him acknowledging me. "This is my friend, Ada," I add, holding Ada's hand.

"Ada," my dad repeats, as if testing the name in his mouth.

His eyes are wide as he stares at Ada, and I almost see the moment he gets lost. He looks at Ada for a long time before looking away.

"I don't know," he says weakly. "I don't know which one of you is my child."

The words crush me, and my grip on Ada's fingers tightens. It's heartbreaking, it's sad, it's horrible. The world is cruel, and my father's condition is crueler. But there's nothing I can fucking do.

Ada leaves my side and kneels down next to my father's bed. The old man's eyes are filled with tears that just won't spill. Even in a moment of weakness, he's as strong as he has always been.

"Hello, Mr. Rhodes. I'm Ada Jones," Ada tells him softly. "Over there is your son, Nathaniel Rhodes. Nate runs a coffee shop called Perk Me Up. I just started working there not too long ago."

She tells him all of this as if he were talking to a regular person, not someone suffering with memory loss, and I like it. My father seems surprised by it, and perhaps it's good for him to finally be treated like a regular person.

Everyone in the facility, including me, his only visitor, treats him like a patient. And I'll bet he's grown tired of that over the years.

"Perk Me Up," my father repeats.

"Yes," Ada adds with a smile. "It's a lovely coffee shop. We just brought out a new flavor of coffee."

"Bah," my Dad shakes his head dismissively. "Only one coffee worth drinking. Black, no sugar, no milk. You kids with those milkshakes you call coffee wouldn't know the right thing."

Ada laughs, a sweet, melodic sound that makes my sore heart swell with relief.

"Well, I happen to love milkshakes," she tells my father.

"But I do love a good pot of plain black coffee too. Especially a fresh roast."

She winks at my dad and the man perks up visibly, giving her a look of new-found interest.

"I like your friend," he tells me, smiling at Ada. "What's her name?"

Ada doesn't falter for a second as she says, "It's Ada Jones, sir."

"I like you," my Dad tells her. "Now will you tell my son, if you ever see him, that he needs to settle down and give me some grandchildren? You seem like a good girl. Will you marry my boy?"

It's like a double hit to the stomach. He forgot I'm here again, and he still doesn't know.

"Excuse me," I say, rushing out of the room.

I can't stay in there a second longer. Everything about it, the cheesy curtains, the floral patterned wallpaper, the shadow of my father in his bed, makes my breaths come in quicker, more ragged.

Ada comes out of the room a moment later and signals to Gail.

"Thank you," Ada tells her.

"Of course." Gail nods. "If anything changes, I'll make sure to call."

Ada leads me out of the locked unit. The door buzzes and beeps as we make our escape. Ada takes my arm and guides me out of the building, out into the last bit of warm sunshine.

We settle on a bench in the gardens, next to a maple tree. I stare at its leaves, ranging from a burnt orange color to a soft honey yellow. I'm doing anything and everything to distract myself, trying not to cry, barf or scream. Maybe all three at the same time.

"It's okay," Ada tells me gently.

She's sitting a few inches away from me on the bench, and for once, I appreciate the distance. I need room to breathe. The walls in that room were starting to close in on me.

"He doesn't know me," I tell her with my voice sounding ragged. "He doesn't know I'm his son. He doesn't know who I am."

We sit in silence for a few long moments, and I pluck a leaf from the ground. This one is a burgundy color, the tone so rich and luxurious it almost looks fake. My fingers trace the veins of the leaf as I try to gather myself once more.

"Did you mean what you said in there?" Ada asks me softly, and I look up into her eyes.

She clears her throat and blushes lightly. For some reason, it makes me smile. I love seeing her get a little vulnerable. I may be a bastard for it, but I love the way I make her blush.

"I mean..." she starts up again. "Am I really your girlfriend?"

She doesn't look at me. Instead, her eyes linger on the lawn littered with fallen leaves in all shades of autumn colors.

I turn to face Ada, gently taking her face in both of my hands, leaving the burgundy leaf on my lap.

"Hey," I say gently, and she finally locks eyes with me for which I am grateful. "Of course I meant it. I thought you knew. I mean, you've been practically living with me..."

"I know, but that doesn't mean we're together," Ada says.

"So you don't want to be?" I ask.

"Fuck no."

I laugh at her vehement reply, and she smiles shyly in return.

"It's just," she begins. "I didn't know if we were even doing the exclusive thing. I wasn't sure what we were doing and I didn't want to ask. We've been so busy..."

"If you think I'm letting you sleep with someone else, I'm gonna spank you so hard you won't be able to walk tomorrow," I tell her half-seriously, half-jokingly, and Ada laughs, shaking her head.

"That's good to know," she tells me.

We sit in companionable silence for a while longer, watching the leaves float to the ground around our feet. When did the leaves change? I feel like summer was only yesterday, but the trees tell me time has passed.

"Does your father have Alzheimer's?" Ada asks, and I stroke her cheek with my thumb before pulling her against me.

She rests her head on my shoulder.

"Dementia," I tell Ada. "It's a long story."

"I have time," she responds in a small voice.

ate

A dark brown leaf flutters to the ground and then skitters along the sidewalk making a crunchy, raspy sound. I watch it for a moment, feeling much like the leaf- powerless and out of control.

"My mom wouldn't have been able to handle this." My voice comes out soft and hoarse at the same time. "I'm so glad she doesn't have to see him like this."

I don't ever tell this story. Fuck knows it's depressing enough. Layla knows some parts of it, and Katy knows a bit, too, but neither knows the whole thing. No one does.

"My mom thought my dad was the strongest, smartest, most handsome man on the planet," I continue, remembering how she used to smile at him when he'd come home. "And for a while he was."

I shuffle my feet in the stack of fallen leaves before continuing with the story.

"My dad's memory started failing a few years ago. It started small and my mother would cover for him. He'd forget his keys or use salt instead of sugar. My mom didn't start to worry until he forgot their anniversary."

I close my eyes, seeing my mother's face.

"He was usually the romantic one. And he didn't realize what day it was. Even after she told him." My voice catches remembering that day. The hurt and pain in my mother's eyes. The panic at knowing something was wrong with him but not knowing what. "That's when she started to worry, but she didn't know what to do. She was a stay-at-home wife who didn't know anything about dementia or even how to pronounce Alzheimer's."

I can remember my mother sitting at the kitchen table, bills scattered about in the yellow light of the lamp. I remember her crying and the frustrated sound of her punching keys on a calculator trying to make everything add up. I remember her frustration trying to talk to Dad and find out what had been paid. It was the only time I remember them fighting.

"She slipped on the ice that winter," I say, my voice emotionless. "The doctors say there wasn't anything we could have done. She went to bed with a headache and never woke up. But at least she didn't have to see him come to this."

"I'm so sorry," Ada whispers, squeezing my hand.

"Dad lived alone for a little while. I didn't know how bad things were. Mom hadn't told me. I think she wanted to keep the illusion of the perfect husband and marriage for as long as she could. I actually thought he'd started drinking and was just drunk all the time because of Mom's death. But he wasn't drunk."

I pause, looking out at the leaves again.

"I started Perk Me Up with so much hope," I tell her. "I put everything I had into it and I took out a loan. It was a big risk, but I thought I could manage. That it would pay out. That my Dad could help and it wouldn't be too bad."

Ada smiles, her hand running down my back in soothing motions.

"Perk Me Up had been open for exactly one month when the police called me. They'd found him wandering around in a town a hundred miles away trying to break into someone's apartment. He thought it was his apartment and had gotten violent with the woman who lived there. She pressed charges."

"Fuck," Ada whispers.

"He was diagnosed with dementia shortly after that." I can still see the doctor's face when he told me. The kindness, sympathy, and sorrow in his eyes. "He wanders and gets lost easily. He tries to go into homes that he thinks are his and then defends them against the 'intruders.' He escaped the first three nursing homes I found for him and they couldn't keep him there safely. That's how we ended up here."

"It's nice here," Ada says, looking around at the autumn leaves and the facility behind us.

"Yeah, but expensive." I run a hand through my hair. "Between the lawsuit with the woman he injured and trying to find a place that could take him, I needed money. Since I was maxed out with the bank loan for the business, I had to go to Frank the Shark."

"I don't know Frank, but I get the feeling he's not the kindly forgiving sort?" Ada asks.

"He will give you money, but if you don't pay it back, he takes everything and then some." I shiver slightly even though the breeze isn't that cold. "I have to pay off that loan as quickly as I can. He'll take the building and everything in it if I don't."

We both look out at the garden around us. It seems so peaceful. It's beautiful out here.

"And do you visit him often?" Ada asks softly. I know she's not talking about Frank.

"Rarely," I tell her honestly. "It's too difficult. He won't speak, and when he does, he doesn't know who I am. I haven't told him about Perk Me Up. Usually, when he knows I'm Nate, he asks about Mom. When he doesn't, there's no point in talking anyway."

I swallow the bitterness and give Ada a long look.

"It's... tough. So I don't tell a lot of people," I admit, and Ada nods knowingly. Ada stares at me, and I can tell how shocked she is by what I'm telling her. I don't open up like this, not ever, and it almost feels therapeutic to tell her what's happened in my past.

"I understand. I mean, I get it," she says. "I don't know what it's like to lose a parent or to have one get sick. I wish there was something I could do to help you."

"I'm so glad you came. He hasn't spoken as much as he has today in... well, at least a year. I haven't been here much. It's... it's just too hard."

I don't mention the guilt threatening to eat me alive for not coming to see my father on a more regular basis. I figure I've already dumped enough information on the poor girl, and she doesn't need to listen to more of my ramblings.

I don't want to frighten her the way my father frightened my mother. I don't need to mention that dementia often has a genetic component.

"Is this why you pushed me away?" Ada motions towards the ward. "Because you don't want me to have to deal with this?"

I nod, unable to say the words.

"I would stay with you always," she whispers. Her head is back on my shoulder so I can't see her face, but my chest tightens with hope.

"I wouldn't want to put you through this pain," I whisper back.

She squeezes my hand. "How can you know joy without knowing sadness? What is light without dark? Pain shows us how deep our love can be. When you care about someone, it doesn't matter where they are. Your father is just not here anymore. That doesn't mean you don't love him any less. It's just harder."

"How'd you get so wise?" I ask her.

She shrugs. "I like to read."

We sit together for long minutes in silence. It isn't awkward, but comforting. I can believe that Ada would stay with me. She already has shown that she can handle my father

"Do you want to go in and say goodbye?" Ada suggests.

I think about it, but finally shake my head. Guilt hangs heavy on my shoulders, but the fear keeping me out here is stronger.

"I don't think I can," I admit. "Not today. Is that alright?"

"Yes," Ada nods.

"Can we go home?" My voice is shaky and embarrassment wraps around me.

"Yes, we can. Wait here while I tell the nurse we're leaving," she says with a smile. She stops and turns. "Would it be okay if I came to visit your dad?"

I smile at her. "You got him to talk to you. You can visit him all you want. Have Gail give you the paperwork and I'll sign that you can visit him."

Ada flashes me a quick grin and heads inside.

The idea of her visiting my father makes my heart feel lighter. He deserves to have someone visit him even if I can't.

A leaf falls from the tree above me and lands in my lap as if placed there. It's a beautiful red maple leaf, bright and vibrant.

Its veins remind me of the people I care about. Ada, me, Layla, Audrey, Jacob, even Sydney. And my dad, too. Perhaps even Katy.

All of the lines form a leaf together. Each of them is an important part of the construction, each of them holding it together. Just like us.

But I still have my friends, and I have my father. I shouldn't give up on him.

Most importantly, I have Ada.

My eyes go up just in time to see her walking towards me down the path from the facility. She smiles and holds up some paperwork for me to sign. Once again, I feel a little lighter, a little more hopeful for what comes next.

She's turned my whole life around, and I honestly believe she's made me a better person. I need to thank her for this. I need to make sure she knows.

I get up, and I watch the burgundy leaf float down to join its own family of fallen friends. They look so beautiful on the lawn, symbolizing autumn and the richness of the season. I smile to myself before following Ada down the path to the parking lot.

I may be broken, but I think I might just be able to piece those puzzles back together, one by one.

*da*

"That's it for class today. Remember that your video projects are due in one month and I expect them to be amazing," Professor Cantrell saya, ending class for the day.

I pack up my ancient laptop and assortment of books. I'm not sure what my video project is going to be on yet, but it will probably have something to do with the coffee shop. I've made so many TikTok videos of our new salted caramel coffee that I'm seeing B-roll coffee footage in my sleep.

I'm having success with the short form video, but this assignment is supposed to be something that lasts at least fifteen minutes. I haven't come up with anything coffee related that is interesting to watch for fifteen minutes yet though.

I sigh, shouldering my bag. I will come up with something. I still have plenty of time to come up with this assignment. I smiled. Maybe I can get Nate to help me out. He has to have some interesting stories that I haven't heard yet, or maybe something about his dad.

I step out of the lecture hall and into the bright autumn sunshine of late morning. Campus has a busy hum this early, but not the manic energy of the afternoon. I love this time of morning, with the crisp air, the bright leaves, and the students all running around with coffee.

An idea for a TikTok hits me and I quickly pull out my phone to catch the students all hurrying to class with coffee in hand. I will add some music, a caption about how Perk Me Up coffee is the best for class, and I will have our next viral video.

I grin, using my camera phone to record the masses walking past with coffees in hand until one person stops in front of me.

"Yes, I'm filming a TikTok, but don't worry, there are no faces in my video. If you'd like to see the final product, please follow Perk Me Up Coffee," I say, not looking at the person but focusing on making sure I get my video shot before everyone disappears into their classes.

"Is this really what you're doing with your life?"

I nearly drop my phone, my entire body going rigid. I swallow hard as my eyes travel up the designer skirt, tailored blazer, and focus on the unhappy face of my mother.

She looks picture perfect, as always. Her makeup is subtle yet classy, and not a single blonde hair out of place in a stylish upswept bun. Her frown barely touches her forehead and I'm sure that her botox person is getting paid well.

"Mom?"

"Well, of course, dear." She smiles, but it doesn't touch her eyes. It has nothing to do with the botox and everything with the fact that she is never happy to see me.

"What are you doing here?" I barely manage to turn off my phone and stuff it into my bag. My hands are shaking and I think I might throw up.

"I'm visiting you, dear," she says, sounding pleasant. "You sound unhappy. I thought you'd be excited to see me."

"Mom, the last time you saw me, you kicked me out of the house and cut me off from all financial assistance. You screamed at Dad. You screamed at me. You told me you never wanted to see me again and that I was dead to you." I'm shocked that my voice stays steady.

"Ada, I did not do any of that," my mother replies, shaking her head. "I know we were both upset, but you are my child. I only want the best for you."

I cross my arms. "You told me that no daughter of yours would end up with a worthless degree. That you refused to be associated with me."

My mother sighs and shakes her head. "I'm sure it felt like I said that to you, but Ada, I love you. I just want what's best for you. I sometimes say things that I don't mean in order to motivate you to do better."

"Motivate me to do better?" I scoff. "I told you that I didn't want to pursue political science and wanted an arts degree. That I wanted to follow my dreams."

"Those dreams won't feed you," my mother replies. "I'm just–"

"My dreams are feeding me, Mom!" I shout at her and instantly regret it.

She frowns. "Your dream is making internet videos for a small town coffee shop on the verge of bankruptcy?"

"It's doing just fine," I say through clenched teeth. "Just like me.""Just fine?" She rolls her eyes and motions to my clothes. "What are you wearing? You look like a homeless person. You're also putting on weight, although at least your skin looks clear."

I want to melt into the ground. Students are starting to stare at us as they pass.

"Mom, this is perfectly acceptable clothing for going to class," I tell her. And it is. I'm wearing jeans and a plain blue t-shirt. Compared to the multitude of students still in pajama pants and sweats, I look downright dressed up.

"Not if you want to be anything in this world. You must dress to impress." My mother frowns at me. "And that necklace. How many times have I told you that it looks worn and simplistic?"

My hand wraps protectively around the silver bird charm. "Dad gave me this."

My mother sighs. "That doesn't mean that you have to wear it. I have a lot of jewelry from him that I don't wear everyday."

"Well, I do," I say stubbornly. I don't tell her that Dad gave it to me to symbolize my freedom when I turned eighteen and could follow my dreams. I don't tell her that he pays for my phone and made sure it was the model with the best camera he could find.

My mother is queen of their house, but my father's small rebellion is the Photoshop subscription he claims is for work but is really for me. He will never openly defy her, but he doesn't agree with her stance that I must be her heir or nothing at all.

"What do you want, Mom?" I ask, suddenly tired. I don't want to have this fight again.

"I came to see you and see if you had come to your senses," she replies, shouldering her cream colored leather purse on her shoulder. She sniffs loudly as she looks around. Her nose wrinkles in disgust. "You belong in a better place than this."

She means I belong in an Ivy League school with a law degree and an old-money boyfriend who will help me win the presidency some day. She would pay my tuition and fees if I went and did what she wanted. I won't do it. I would rather be broke, working in a coffee shop, and up to my eyeballs in student loan debt than be the doll she wants.

I am my own person. I choose my own fate. I will find my own happiness.

"I am happy here, Mom."

"Darling, I know you. You aren't happy here. You're just happy that you're making me angry," she informs me. "You will be happier where you belong, and that's not here. You're so much more than this."

I bristle, but this is an argument she and I have had so many times it's a broken record. We'll fight. She'll say that she just wants me to rise to my full potential. I'll say that I want to take photos. She'll say I can do that as a hobby, but that I really should get a real career.

We'll end up yelling. Nothing will be accomplished.

"It was nice to see you, Mom." I shoulder my bag and walk around her. I am no longer a child. I don't have to stand there and listen to her tell me what I should want. I will leave this conversation before she can guilt me into anything I don't want to do.

"I know you're seeing someone."

My feet stop moving. Anxiety and dread make my feet heavy. How could she know? I can't help but wonder if she'd like him. I know Dad would, but Mom doesn't like anyone.

"He's not a good fit for you, Ada." My mother sounds kind and gentle. "He may seem wonderful, but what do you really know about him? Do you really belong with him?"

I can't help it. I think of all the doubts around Nate and I's relationship. The age difference. The wage difference and the fact that he's my boss. The fact that he's had so many life experiences and I have had so few.

"Have you met him?" I ask. My voice quivers. I shouldn't care, but I'm afraid of what my mother thinks.

She sighs. "He's too old for you. And while I do appreciate that he is successful, I have to wonder at what cost. Does he support your dreams? I don't know if he is ready for the life you will want to lead."

"He does. He supports my art," I tell her. She manages not to roll her eyes.

"And are you ready for his life? He is not going to be an easy man to live with. He will not be able to change his habits easily," she warns. "Are you really worthy of him?"

"I really hope you didn't travel all the way out here just for this, Mom," I tell her, struggling to keep my composure. I don't want her to know how close she is to hitting my emotions.

"Is he really what you want? Or is he just what is convenient?" my mother asks. I hate that the question echoes and rattles in my mind. I hate that it's one I've asked myself.

That is my mother's poison gift. She is able to twist my own thoughts into her desires. She is able to always make me want to please her. To make her proud.

I love Nate. Or at least I think I do. We haven't said it to one another yet, but I want to. I want to tell him how I feel when I'm around him.

Happy. Safe. Content. Wanted.

We are a good pair together, no matter what my mother wants me to think.

I cross my arms and face my mother. I am strong. I do not need my mother butting into my relationship or my life. "Thank you for your concern, Mom. I hope you have a safe trip home."

She looks at me with eyes that are angry and sad at the same time. She thinks I'm wasting my life and giving up on my potential. She has such big dreams for me, but they are her dreams, not mine. I don't want to have a law degree, become a senator, and then run for president.

I just want to take pictures. I want to show the beauty of the world the way that only I can see it.

"You will change your mind, dear," my mother calls out to me as I walk away. "This isn't something you can just forget."

I ignore her, walking at a brisk pace that wants to turn into a run. I wish that I didn't want to run back to her, curl up in her arms, and want to promise to be good if only she'll love me. I wish we could be a different kind of mother and daughter.

She's right that I can't just forget about her though. Family ties and family desires aren't something anyone can just forget. You'd have to lose everything in your mind to have that happen. Family, and the family that we make, is everything in this world.

I stop so quickly that my hair flies into my face. The student walking behind me nearly runs me over, but I don't care. Inspiration is flowing through me, lighting up every nerve with bolts of lightning. My fingers itch to get behind a camera.

I check to make sure I have my camera in my bag and then I take off running to my car. I need to see Nate's dad about helping with my project.

CHAPTER 28

ate

"Nate, I need you to do this," Ada tells me, handing me the phone.

I sigh. I hate doing things this way.

All around the coffee shop, no one else seems to notice or mind the digital world crowding around them. My shop is full of teens and young college kids all talking about the TikToks that brought them here.

"It's an online signature," she continues, shrugging like it doesn't matter. "I don't see why you don't like it. It makes everything easier."

"Signing on paper so there is a paper trail makes things easier," I grumble, swirling my finger on the screen. It doesn't look anything like my real signature but no one at the facility will care.

"It saves trees," Ada informs me, taking the phone back

and tucking it in her pocket. "It's good for the environment."

I hold my tongue. If only Ada knew how much was "good for the environment" that had absolutely nothing to do with making the world a better place but simply about making money.

She was too innocent for her own good. The world hadn't made her bitter and cynical of everything yet. She's still happy to put her entire life on line in pictures and signatures. I want hard copies of everything.

"Thank you for signing these," she tells me. "I really appreciate it."

I shrug. She wants to take some video of my dad for a class. I don't think she'll get anything useful out of him, but then again, she did make him talk while we were there. He had smiled and spoken to her, which is more than he does for anyone else.

I shake my head. My father seems to love Ada nearly as much as I do.

"I just hope it works for you," I tell her. "My dad isn't exactly a movie star."

"He's perfect," she tells me, her eyes going far away. I can see the wheels turning in her head. It's what she does when she's planning a shot or figuring out how to edit something together. I've seen her make that face when she makes a complicated coffee order.

"If you say so." I shrug again.

Her eyes focus back to me. "So, what are you up to today? You look very fancy."

I look down at my suit and tie. I do look far more dressed up than the ragged assortment of college kids surrounding us in the cafe.

"I'm paying off half the loan today," I reply with a grin.

Her eyes go wide. "Really? You have enough?"

"It's all thanks to you and your TikToks." I lean over and kiss her cheek. "You and your damn phone app is saving my hide."

She giggles. "One of these days I'll get you to make a video yourself. They're actually pretty fun."

I make a face. "Nope. Not doing that techy stuff. I'd rather be in the real world."

She rolls her eyes and shakes her head, but keeps a smile on her face.

"So, half the loan? Not the whole thing?" she asks.

I sigh. "It's a big loan. And if I default, Frank gets this entire building. He's wanted it for years. I think he was really hoping this place would fail and he'd get to take over."

"And you went to that guy for a loan?" Ada raises an eyebrow at me.

"He was the only person I could go to," I explain. "But if I pay off half of the loan, he can't take the shop. It'll also decrease the interest into something more manageable."

"Frank the Loan Shark gives good interest rates?" Ada asks.

"He's a shark, not stupid. If he doesn't keep the deals, he won't get the loans."

"So why not wait and just pay the whole thing off?" Ada asks. "Or keep paying what you are now but save up a lot so you can pay it off all at once?"

"I considered all those options," I reply. She's so young. She doesn't understand loans, especially these slightly shady ones. I don't want to explain it because it will make me feel like a teacher. "This is the best one. Trust me."

"Okay." She shrugs and picks up her camera, playing with some settings. I can tell she's not thrilled with my answer, but I'm not about to change my ways. "I have some more ideas to get the rest of the loan paid off. Especially if it means you won't lose the building."

I raise an eyebrow. "That sounds interesting. You'll have to tell me about them when I get back."

She grins. "Only if you do a TikTok for me."

I sigh. "Then it will just be a surprise then."

Her smile holds but the corner of her right eye twitches slightly. I can't keep up with all these social media platforms. They change yearly and all they want is everyone's data to sell off to the highest bidder. Ada is welcome to it. I don't want it.

I stand up from our table and kiss her cheek. She smiles at me and wishes me good luck as I head out the door.

Outside it's late morning and fall has fully arrived. The air is crisp and cool with the scent of leaves and apples. Everyone is wearing sweatshirts and hats while still enjoying the orange glow of sunshine before winter comes.

I walk the downtown streets, finding my way to Frank's place of business. It doesn't look like much on the outside, but Frank secretly runs this town. I've heard that the mayor owes him money along with most of the businesses on Main Street. He basically owns the University football team and has ties to nearly every profitable professor on campus.

The building is a small, but nice looking glass building. "Frank Meyes, Attorney" shimmers in golden lettering on the outside doors and windows. Inside, his secretary sits at a big desk and soft music plays overhead.

Anyone would think that he was just a successful small town lawyer. No one would suspect the businesses that went on in this building.

His secretary waves me into Frank's office without even looking up from her phone. I hope she's watching Ada's TikToks about our coffee. The place smells thickly of apple spice air freshener to the point I wish someone would open a window.

"Nate, how nice to see you," Frank says, not rising from his chair. His office makes mine look like a cubicle. He has a huge oak desk, bookshelves everywhere, and expensive leather furniture that's heavy and incredibly masculine.

Frank is older than my father, but he doesn't look it. His dark hair is artfully swirled with gray, giving him a distinguished look. He doesn't look worn like my father does. I wish Frank looked like the shark he is, but he doesn't. He's handsome and trustworthy, with a strong jaw and an easy smile.

"I came to bring you this," I say, pulling out the cashier's check from my pocket. I set it on his desk and push it toward him with a finger.

Frank looks down at it. "What? That's not what you owe me."

"It's half of what's left," I tell him. "That's my payment this month."

Frank doesn't reach for the check. "You'll still have to pay me next month. This doesn't give you more time."

I feel my Adam's apple bob as I swallow. The mood in the room has gone from cheery to dangerous.

"Of course. I just want to pay it off as soon as possible. I want to get your money back to you," I tell him.

Frank looks at the check again, but doesn't pick it up. He looks at the check like it's got a curse on it. I suppose it does to him. If I didn't pay this, he would get the building he wants.

"Where'd you get the money?" he asks. A cruel smile curves his handsome features. "Finally take Katy up on paying for things?"

"No. Katy and I aren't together. That came from my shop," I reply. "Business is booming."

"No, it came from the TikToks bringing people to your shop." Frank laughs. It is a nice laugh, but it makes me feel uncomfortable. His eyes meet mine. "Whoever you have running your social media is a genius."

"I agree." I don't want to tell him about Ada. I don't want Ada anywhere near this man. He will stop at nothing to get what he wants.

"Well, whoever it is, send them my way if they want a real job," Frank says, leaning back in his chair. "I'd love to have them on my team."

"I'll let them know."

"I'd be happy to knock a few bucks off your loan if you'll share your media manager," Frank pushes. "I know it's not Layla. It's someone new. Who is it?"

"Just a random college kid," I lie. "I'll let him know that his skills are appreciated."

"You do that." Frank's smile fades. "Thanks for the payment, Nate. See you next month."

"Hopefully, I'll be paying it off next month." I don't know why I say this. I don't have the cash flow to pay it off, but I wish I did. I wish I could be free of this man and this loan hanging on my neck. If I don't pay him, he takes my business, my home, and my dreams.

Frank's eyes widen just a bit. "Well. That would be something. Maybe you'd still be interested in selling the building?"

I shake my head. "Not with business booming the way it is. I know you want that building, but it's in just too good a spot to give it up."

Frank nods. "I'm still mad your old man beat me to buying it. But, I don't hold grudges. Maybe one day it will finally be mine."

He smiles, but this time, there is a feral quality that makes me shiver.

"How is your old man, Nate?"

I freeze for only a second before putting on a big smile.

"He's actually doing better. The doctor's think his new medicine is really promising," I lie my ass off. "It's a medical miracle."

"I can't wait to read about it in the next edition of the New England Journal of Medicine," Frank replies sarcastically.

"Good to see you, Frank," I reply. I motion to the check with my head. "Take your time cashing that. There's plenty of money in the account."

I leave the office, walking confidently. I smile politely to the secretary, but her face is buried in her phone and she doesn't acknowledge my presence. I head out into the cool sunshine, taking in a gasp of clean air.

Dread and relief both pull at me. Dread that I have to pay off the rest of this loan as quickly as I can. I hadn't expected Frank to react so negatively to me paying the loan. Yet, I am relieved that I have half of it paid off. With a little help, it might be possible to pay it all off by the end of the year.

I let myself have that dream for a moment. The dream that Ada's videos would free us both and we could live a life together that was completely ours. A life without Frank hiding in the background.

I start walking. This payment was only possible because of Ada. Her knowledge of social media and her caramel recipe. I owe this all to her. I have to tell her. I have a new respect for what she's done. She may be younger, but she's smarter than I am. I am so lucky to have her.

I'm going to make a TikTok for her to prove it. I'll even do one of the stupid dances if she wants.

CHAPTER 29

*N*ate

Fall is about watching Rocky run around, rummaging in piles of leaves.

Fall is about sipping Salted Caramel lattes with Ada while we read the morning paper.

Fall is about the visits to my father and sitting beneath the ever-changing maple tree in the garden.

Fall is about dinners with my friends at my place, warming ourselves up in the old fireplace in my apartment.

Fall is about falling in love with Ada more and more every day.

In all my years, I've never been so happy. It took a young woman for me to find my joy.

"Hey, penny for them," Ada grins at me, putting her necklace on in front of the mirror in the dining room.

She's wearing a baggy sweater and leggings that drive me wild. I love the way her cute ass looks and how soft the fabric is when I spank her butt.

I smile and walk over to her, abandoning my coffee on the dining room table. We've upgraded since my first dinner party, and now it can seat ten people comfortably. It's a little too big for the small space, but I'd rather have the table. I will have to figure out a remodel for the apartment eventually.

"I was thinking," I tell her.

She looks at me as I fix her necklace and straighten it. It's still early morning, but she looks radiant and so lovely. I still can't believe that someone as young and beautiful as her would want to spend any time with someone as old and crotchety as me.

"You're not old," she says, rolling her eyes and I realize I've spoken out loud.

"I'm older than you," I reply.

"Yeah, and so is Brad Pitt. I'd still be interested," she tells me.

I can't help but smile.

"So, what were you thinking about?" she asks again. Her smile is so sweet that I want to kiss her and taste it.

"I was thinking of a remodel of the cafe," I admit. "I shouldn't. We don't have the money yet, but–"

"You need more kitchen space. We keep bumping elbows making the caramel," Ada interrupts. "And more seating. If we can move the cabinet that holds all the tea closer to the window, we can fit in another bar seating area."

"I can tell you haven't given this a moment's thought," I tease her.

She blushes. "I love the coffee shop just the way it is, but it is old and could use some improvements."

"Old like me?" I ask her, raising an eyebrow.

She blushes harder, but taps her lips like she's thinking. "Well, I suppose there are some improvements you can make."

"Such as?" There is a fake warning in my voice as I cross my arms.

She looks me up and down as if evaluating. She purses her lips and then shakes her head. "Yup. Definite improvements." She shrugs, bringing her eyes to mine. "You have too many clothes on."

I laugh, caught off guard. I'd expected something like I needed to be two inches taller or have less gray hair.

She grins, flashing me an innocent look that I know is anything but. "Luckily, there is an easy remedy."

"And you don't have anywhere you have to be?" I ask her, standing up. I should go to the office. I should go work. There are a million things that I should do.

But I'm going to do her instead.

She grins at the look on my face, knowing that she's won. Without a word, she turns and sashays into the bedroom, knowing that I am watching her perfect ass swish with every step. She must know how those leggings make me think deliciously dark thoughts.

I follow her into the bedroom, mesmerized by her leggings. I catch up to her and spank her on the ass hard enough that there is a smack even through the fabric.

She yips with surprise, but her eyes are alight with lust when she turns to find me. She keeps her butt away from my hands, however, unwilling for me to spank her again.

"You started it," I tell her, coming up and putting my

hands on her hips. "Wearing those leggings around the house. You know what it does to me."

She grins. "You just need more self control."

"I have plenty. I waited until you asked," I reply.

She chuckles. "Then I should have asked earlier."

She kisses me, her mouth warm with the taste of coffee. I want to bury myself in her. If I could be out of my clothes and inside her warmth I would do so in a heartbeat. As much as I love our foreplay, as much as I love touching her and making her come undone with my fingers and mouth, I love being inside of her more.

I love claiming her as my own. I love losing myself inside of her and finding my heart in the process. She makes me feel like myself. When I am with her, I know who I want to be and who I can be.

I can be her hero. I can give her the rapture and joy she deserves.

I slide my hand down her hip, grabbing her amazing ass through the fantastic leggings.

"I wish there were a way we didn't have to take these off," i whisper, gently rubbing the spot I just smacked. "I love the way you look in them."

"I think you like the way I look out of them just as much," she replies. She grins up at me as she slides the leggings free of her long legs, leaving her in a shirt and panties. My mouth goes dry watching her.

I can't believe she is mine. I can't believe that she is here with me and that I am this lucky.

She pulls the sweater over her head, leaving her in just a simple cotton bra and panties.

"You're still wearing too many clothes," she informs

me. She cocks her head. "Do you need help taking them off?"

I nod and she giggles. She comes to me, helping peel the t-shirt up and over my head. It catches on my elbows, trapping my arms overhead and blindfolding me. She delights in my capture, taking the opportunity to kiss me while I can't see her.

Even blindfolded, I know she is beautiful.

I fling the t-shirt to the floor and she goes for my pants. The slide off easily and I kick them free until all I have is my briefs on.

She looks down at me and bites her lip. She slides the bird charm along the chain as she licks her lips, her eyes focused on what she wants. Slowly, her gaze comes back up to mine.

I don't wait for her to speak. I reach for her. She kisses me and I undo the clasps of her bra, letting if fall away. She wriggles free of it so that she can press her chest against mine.

She is soft where I am hard. She is young where I am old. She is flexible where I am rigid. She is mine.

I slide a finger down to the waistband of her underwear. They are just simple cotton ones today, but the simplicity of them is actually more alluring than the fancy lace. These tell me that she is comfortable.

I slide my hand into them, pressing my thumb against the small nub of pleasure and working my fingers against her entrance. She moans slightly, letting her head tilt back. I kiss her throat, watching the fluttering pulse in her neck as I begin to make her feel good.

Carefully, I lower her onto the bed. I strip the panties off her, no longer wanting them in my way as my hand once agains seeks out her pleasure. Her hips arch into my touch, and she grabs at her breasts, pinching her own nipples to enhance her pleasure.

I love to watch her like this. I love to watch her writhe and find bliss at my touch.

It doesn't take me long to find the exact rhythm and tempo that drives her wild. I'm learning her body like a musician learns an instrument, slowly turning into a master that can coax the most beautiful music from it at a moments notice.

I love when her body tenses. Her legs shake and her mouth forms a small "o". I know that she would hate her o-face. That she would feel self conscious and silly about it, but I think watching her make that face is the sexiest thing in the entire world.

I love it when she comes on my fingers, her body finding pleasure in my touch. I wait until the rhythm pulses pounding through her body slow and stop before standing to go to the nightstand.

"Stop," she says, grabbing my wrist. Her eyes meet mine. "You don't need that."

"I don't?" I raise an eyebrow.

She smiles. "I'm on birth control. And I trust you."

That simple phrase makes my heart melt.

She trusts me.

I kiss her and she guides me into her, gasping as I fill her. I gasp too. She is so warm and wet. Her body wraps around and caresses me like she was made explicitly for me. Her back arches, drawing me in further.

I groan in delight, diving into her. Our hips find the tempo that best suits us, our bodies finding passion and pleasure. Every stroke inside of her is a step closer to heaven. Every thrust is another chance at finding release that only she can grant me.

"Get on your stomach," I tell her, pulling out of her sweet warmth and immediately regretting it.

I'm glad she flips over quickly, raising that perfect ass and wiggling it to tempt me to get right back in.

I slide in, pressing one hand on her low back. This new position is intense and powerful, for both of us. I am in control here, but she is able to rock her hips and cause more pleasure in me than I think she can understand.

She squeezes around me. I slap her ass, this time the sound crisp and clear without the leggings in the way. She yelps into the pillow and then begs me to do it again.

I do it once more before I know I'm going to lose myself to her. I want to focus on how good she feels. I grab her hips, feeling her soft curves under my palms. Her body rises to meet me, urging me on.

"Come in me," she gasps, her voice ragged and full of need that only I can satisfy.

I claim her. I want her to always be mine, and so I fill her with my essence, marking her as my own. It is a primal need that I give into, one that I can only satisfy with her. I never have sex without a condom, but I trust her.

I trust her.

Pleasure, lust, and raw need explode out of me and she accepts it all. She takes all of me with only a gaps of plea-sure and a shuddering of her own pleasure as I lose myself in her.

It feels so good. So right.

I slide out of her, and she immediately folds into my

embrace. We lay side by side like spoons in a drawer. I am the big spoon, keeping her safe and warm.

"I love you," I whisper in her ear. I don't have to think about the words. They just come naturally.

I can feel her smile as she nestles deeper into my arms.

"I love you, too."

My heart soars.

We are complete.

CHAPTER 30

*N*ate

"Well, Rocky, what should we do this evening?" I ask my dog. Ada is supposed to be off doing school things today-going to class and working on her big project, so I'm taking the opportunity to work at home by myself. Or rather, with Rocky.

Rocky looks over at me, his brown eyes big and sleepy. He's getting curlier and cuter every day, the poodle in him coming out. Pretty soon I'm going to have to take him to the groomer and have him cleaned up so he can see out his eyes without fur blocking them.

I chuckle, thinking that I should have him groomed to look like a traditional poodle with the poofy tail and silly hair. Ada would probably love it.

Rocky looks toward the door, his ears perked and hopeful for a third walk.

I shake my head. "Your options are to nap on the floor by the fire or nap on your bed in the bedroom."

Rocky yawns and pads over to the couch. He hops up and promptly sprawls out in a very undignified position that looks horribly uncomfortable. He sighs contentedly and then starts to snore.

I roll my eyes and head to the small desk in the corner of the living room.

I don't have much work to do today, apart from looking at some applications for Perk Me Up. We need to hire another barista. It's becoming clear we need more help, and now that we have even more people coming in, we really need all the employees we can get. The cafe is busy enough now that we need two people making coffee while one runs the cash register.

It's a good problem to have.

I file through the applications, all of them blending before my eyes. They all seem the same. Finally, one of them catches my eye and I pull it out.

Jacob's name is neatly printed at the top of the application complete with resume and cover letter.

I never knew he wanted to work at Perk Me Up. He hasn't mentioned it to me once. I wonder what made him want to work here.

Nathaniel, I know this might seem a little weird, it reads.

But I'd love to work at Perk Me Up. I have some extra time now that I'm a senior, and I really enjoy the atmosphere. Some extra money would be nice, but I'm mostly excited about spending more time in the cafe. I hope you'll consider my application - perhaps I would be a good fit. Jacob.

I laugh to myself, immediately deciding to give him the job. I don't care if it makes me a dick since he's a friend of ours. He'd be the perfect fit. Besides, he spends most of his time in Perk Me Up already. I might as well start paying him.

I pick up my cell to call Jacob and give him the good news, when a knock on the door interrupts me. I get up with a frown, hoping Ada hasn't forgotten something. She's supposed to be in class and then she's working on her big project. She won't tell me what it's about, but she's putting her heart into it.

"Hey, babe," I say, heading for the door. "I hope you don't end up being late…"

I open the door, but Ada isn't standing there.

Instead, a woman stands before me, perhaps in her late forties, very beautiful in that classic way. She's got blonde hair carefully wrapped up in a small chignon, blue eyes and is wearing an expensive pantsuit I'm sure I've seen in last month's Vogue. She's absolutely stunning, and she's the spitting image of my girlfriend in thirty years.

"Hello," I say slowly, giving her a onceover.

She's clutching a Lady Dior bag in her hands. She's playing with a silver bead on it the same way Ada plays with her necklace when she's nervous.

"Are you Nathaniel Rhodes?" she finally asks me in a dignified and confident voice.

"That would be me," I reply warily. "How can I help you, ma'am?"

"I'm… I'm Ada's mother," she tells me.

"That much is clear," I smile at her. "You two look so much alike."

She doesn't smile back, so I step aside, motioning for her to follow me.

"Would you like to come in?" I ask her.

She waits a long moment before nodding and finally walking into my apartment.

She takes a long look at the interior, the high ceilings, the modern decor, the fire burning in my fireplace.

"Excuse me while I just put another log on," I tell her, sensing that she needs a moment to collect herself.

I walk over to the fireplace and put another piece of wood on the dying fire. I take the poker and make sure it catches on fire, the slow burn bringing a scent of pines and home to my nose. Rocky is a terrible guard dog and doesn't even bother to wake up.

I take my time, but when I turn back to face the woman, she's still standing in the exact same spot.

"Please, come in," I ask her pleasantly, and still she stands still.

Not waiting for her, I walk over to the dining table and stack the job applications, putting them away in a drawer. Rocky lifts his head curiously from his spot on the couch, then tucks it between his paws sleepily.

"Would you like a cup of coffee?" I ask Mrs. Jones, and that seems to wake her up from her thoughts.

"That would be nice, thank you," she nods, finally moving a step forward.

"Great," I reply. "Why don't you take a seat at the table and I'll make us both a cup."

I turn my back to her and walk into the kitchen, pulling out everything I need to make the beverages. I decide to go with Ada's Salted Caramel, making it like we always do at home, with her family recipe.

"You know, Ada taught me how to prepare this caramel," I tell her pleasantly as I wash my hands and prep the kitchen.

She only stares in front of her like she doesn't even hear what I'm saying. I pour the sugar in a small saucepan and prepare the coffee.

"Are you sleeping with her?" she suddenly asks me.

My whole body tenses up, and I turn around to look at her. "Excuse me?"

"Ada," she says calmly. "Are you sleeping with my daughter?"

"I don't understand…" I begin to say, but she cuts me off by waving her hand dismissively. She's shaking, trembling like a leaf, yet she seems determined to say what she has come here to tell me.

"I assume you are," she says. "Which means you've corrupted her already."

"Excuse me?" I ask again, looking at her with shock in my eyes.

The woman pulls out her wallet and looks right at me.

"I've done some research," she tells me calmly. "I know your little coffee shop is in trouble. Or used to be, whatever. I also know about your father, Nathaniel Rhodes. I know his medical bills are only going to pile up and soon, you won't be able to handle it all, darling."

"I don't see how that's any of your business," I reply in a clipped tone.

"Whatever concerns Ada is my business," she tells me calmly.

"I don't think so," I shake my head. "You kicked her out of your home, out of your mind. Out of your cold heart."

I want to say something meaner, something that will really offend her, but I bite my tongue instead. I'm not going to get into a fight with this woman, as badly as she wants me to.

"I know everyone has a price, Nathaniel," she says sweetly, pulling a cheque book from her wallet. "So why don't you tell me yours?"

I'm so shocked I can only stare at her as she pulls out a pen too, clicks it open and poises it over the cheque. She gives me an expectant look.

"Get out," I say softly.

"Excuse me?" She actually has the guts to sound surprised.

"Get the fuck out of my apartment," I repeat, louder this time.

She stares at me for a long time, then throws the pen at my head with all her strength. I barely manage to duck out of the way as she gets up, walking up to me.

"My daughter deserves more than you. I have big plans for her."

"You think you can magically make her what you want if you remove me from the equation?" I spit at her.

"It's the first step," she says with a pleasant smile.

"You're disgusting," I tell her.

"I'm sure we both know who the disgusting one here is," she tells me. "You're the only one who should be ashamed of himself, Nathaniel Rhodes. She's still a child. You are a grown man."

"Get out," I repeat, but this time, my voice is shaky. "Please, just… leave."

"Alright." She laughs softly and heads for the door.

Thank fuck for that.

"I have my ways, Nate," she says cryptically before finally exiting my apartment.

And all there is left is Rocky whimpering and the scent of burnt caramel in the air.

da

"A little more to the left," Audrey tells me. "Just a scooch."

"How much is a scooch?" I ask, shifting the painting along the wall a half an inch.

"Not that much, that's at least two scooches," Audrey informs me. "Bring it back a little."

I move it slowly until Audrey shouts that it's perfect. I mark the wall and set the painting down, shaking out my arms.

"I got this one," Jacob informs me, coming up with a hammer and nails. I happily move to the side, watching as Jacob gets up on the shop's small step stool and hangs the new art on the wall.

"These look so good," Layla says, coming up to join us. "I'm so glad you convinced Nate to let us hang local art in here."

"Well…" I grimace.

"You didn't ask?" Layla sounds surprised.

"Better to beg forgiveness than ask permission," I tell her. "But I think it'll be really good for the store. It makes it more local and the response to the first few photos was amazing. Nate didn't even notice that I'd switched them out."

"Yeah, he was too busy making moon eyes at you," Audrey informs me. She makes a kissy face and laughs. I stick my tongue out at her.

"I think he's going to notice this one," Dustin says, cocking his head to look at it better. "I mean, it is a picture of him."

"He'll probably be oblivious," Layla replies.

I laugh. Hanging on the wall is the picture I took of him on our first outing. I printed it in black and white and it looks just as good as I thought it would. Nate is outlined on Main Street with storm clouds behind him but a smile on his face.

"Still, I like it," Layla announces. "Local artwork hanging on the walls, good coffee, and an even better staff. I think this place is coming up in the world."

"And tonight is going to prove it," Audrey agrees. "Is everything ready?"

"The invites are out and we're getting a huge response on all our social media," I reply. "It's going to be a full house tonight."

"Then we better get started before Nate gets here and gets bossy," Layla replies. "The event starts in just a few hours."

We hang ribbons, streamers, and white fairy lights all around the shop. It feels festive and bright as we decorate the tables, chairs, and counter with apples, pumpkins, and fake leaves. By the time we're done it looks like Hobby Lobby exploded an autumn sale inside the store.

"Do you think it's too much?" Layla asks me.

"Maybe, but isn't that kind of the point? To make a statement?" I pull out my camera and start snapping photos and videos to make into TikToks for later. "Besides, it looks good on camera."

Layla gives me a quick side-hug before going to help Sydney hang some more lights.

It really feels like we've all come together again. Like we're our own little family, working on a party for one of our own. And it feels damn good to finally be accepted like this, to feel like I honest-to-God belong somewhere.

It feels like home.

"Guys, Nate is coming!" Jacob warns, hurrying into the shop.

Nate steps into the shop, looking like a million bucks. He's brushed his hair back, and he's wearing one of the suits I love. It's a dark gray and shows off his broad shoulders. He has a crisp black shirt underneath that gives him an air of mystery. He looks successful and ready to run his business.

"Wow," he says, looking around. "You guys did amazing."

I grin and run over to him. "Let me show you everything we have set up."

"First, you have something on your cheek," he says, wiping his thumb against my cheekbone. He pulls back his finger and I can see that it's covered in glitter.

"Oh. I must have bumped the glitter ball," I mumble, pointing to a very shiny decoration hanging by the door. I realize that I must look like a complete mess. Where Nate is all dressed up and professional, I'm wearing ripped jeans, a worn out sweatshirt, and a ponytail that needed fixing two hours ago.

"Over here, we have the silent auction items," Layla interjects. "We got businesses all up and down Main Street to chip in. The restaurants have specialty dinners that aren't on the menu, the bakery is offering a custom cake, and the Gem and Rock store has donated an amazing crystal."

Layla is the one that got all the other businesses to chip in. She worked hard and used a lot of her amazing charm to get the very generous donations for the silent auction.

"Here is our stage," I say, presenting the makeshift stage Jacob conjured up using all his music connections. "Live music all night long."

"And these?" Nate walks over to a wall of mugs and coffee supplies. Many have humorous quotes about coffee and the need to have more of it. There's also a bottle of our salted caramel syrup for those who want to make the coffee flavor at home.

"Those are on sale tonight," I tell him. "I have a friend that makes coffee tumblers and mugs as a business. She's splitting the profits with us on everything we sell or commission tonight."

"This is amazing," Nate says, standing in the center of the cafe and looking around in amazement. "I can't believe you did all of this."

I beam at him. "Well, it was a group effort."

He takes me in his arms, kissing me even though I'm

covered in glitter and grime from setting up. I can smell his pine and coffee scent that makes my knees go wobbly.

"Thank you," he breathes into our kiss. "You have no idea how much this means to me."

I grin up at him, leaning back so I can look at his face. "By the way you're kissing me, I have a pretty good idea."

"You don't get to keep all the money, you know," Audrey reminds him. "All the proceeds from the silent auction go to the animal shelter. And we're paying the bands."

"Yes, but we're selling coffee, food, and fun things," Layla reminds her. She grins, looking a little dangerous. "We're going to make a mint tonight. I can feel it."

Nate laughs, his arms still wrapped around me. "You all are amazing."

He squeezes me as he says it, and it feels like he's saying that I'm amazing. I stand a little bit taller.

Ever since my mother's visit, I've been feeling off kilter. I watch Nate, seeing if he looks at me differently after meeting the crazy that is my mom. Her need for me to succeed doesn't seem to bother him.

But I still feel our age difference. I love Nate, but he's so successful now. Why would he want to date a broke college kid who plans on taking pictures and being an "influencer" for their life goals? I'm not sure I'd want to date me.

I know that I shouldn't let my mother get into my head like this, but her words keep slipping in.

Is he really what you want? Or is he just what is convenient?

da

The place is packed. I've never seen Perk Me Up so full. Everyone is buying coffee and cookies, mugs and art, and the silent auction is going gangbusters. The animal shelter is going to be well stocked by the end of the night, and so is Nate.

I can practically feel Nate's tension sliding from him as he watches the way the community is rallying around him. Every person that comes up to him tells him how much they enjoy the shop and that they're trying to come around more.

Seeing him happy makes me happy. All I want to do is touch him, but we're in a crowded room. He slides his hand along my backside as we walk, and I look over at him. He grins, giving me a naughty wink.

Throughout our night, he finds ways to touch me. A

kiss on the neck when no one is looking, a casual brush of his hand across bare skin. Within a couple of hours, I am hot and bothered by his constant teasing.

I don't know how I will wait until after this party is over to have him. All I can think about is how good he will feel deep inside of me, the way his face will relax, and how good we'll both feel with the stress relief we both need.

"Ada, I need you to come help me in the kitchen for a second," Nate says as Jacob introduces the next band up on the stage.

I wonder if we need more caramel. We've been flying through cups of it. I'd had a few bottles made to sell and they were gone within the first hour. I wish I'd made more to sell given how popular they've been.

I smile and follow him into the kitchen. It's slightly quieter back here, the band muffled by the door and the stainless steel fridges.

A stainless steel fridge that I am currently pressed up against as Nate kisses me like he's been waiting all night to do so. His thigh slides between my legs and I grind against him, moaning softly.

"I've wanted to do that all night," Nate tells me, still pinning to the fridge. I can feel his desire pressed up against my thigh. He's hard and long and ready to go.

"Just that?" I ask, innocently fluttering my eyelashes at him. I love the way his pupils suddenly dilate and his cock twitches against me. "I was hoping for more."

"Yeah?" It seems he's lost the ability to speak and I grin. I push him off of me and grab his hand, leading him back toward his office.

"I think we need to discuss something in private," I say,

deliberately swishing my hips as I walk in front of him. He follows behind me like a puppy.

We pretend to have decency as we make the short walk from the kitchen to his office, but the moment the door is shut, he's on me.

We're kissing hard, tasting one another as if we've never done this dance before.

"Fuck, baby," Nate breathes.

"I know," I tell him, reaching for his belt buckle. I have it undone, his pants around his ankles and his cock in my fist. I want his hard length inside of me and I don't want to wait.

I sit on the edge of the desk, hiking my skirt up around my waist. Before I manage to beg him for it though, he pulls down my undies, nearly ripping them in the process. I don't even care. I just want him in me.

"I'm so glad you planned all of this," Nate murmurs, rubbing the tip of his cock against my entrance, teasing me with what he has to offer.

"It… ahhh… It was really a joint effort," I manage to choke out, barely able to contain the need to feel him. "Please…"

He dips just the tip inside of me, teasing me with the pleasure he could offer. I buck my hips trying to force him inside of me, but he just chuckles and pulls away.

"You want it?" he asks, his breath tickling the tiny hairs on my neck as he whispers in my ear. He presses against me again, just the tip.

"Yes," I whimper. "I want you."

He slams deep inside of me.

I want to cry out, but I know that I'll still be heard even over the band outside. Instead, I bite down on his shoulder, using his body to muffle my scream of pleasure.

He goes hard and fast, the two of us using our pleasure to release the stress of the evening.

I balance on the edge of his desk, holding on for dear life as he thrusts so deeply into me that I can't help but cry out and cling to him.

It reminds me so much of our first night together, the way he'd felt inside of me while I balanced on the dryer. Only this is better. It's harder and faster, more full of need. We aren't nervous or shy, there is no embarrassment anymore.

Just lust. Desire. And so much pleasure that I'm sure I'm about to explode.

"Come for me," I gasp, fisting his shirt in my hands. "I need it."

I know the telltale signs that he's about to come. His breath changes. His muscles tense. I can feel him inside of me, swelling and filling with his seed. I want it all.

He groans, thrusting erratically as he loses himself to me. His climax pushes me into one of my own, my body milking his for my pleasure and giving him more at the same time.

We hold there for a moment, my legs wrapped around his bare ass, my skirt around my waist.

And just then, at the worst possible moment, the office door flies open.

_da_

"Nate, I thought I'd…" a female voice says.

We both turn towards the voice like two deer caught in the headlights. Whoever it is has a perfect view of Nate's bare ass with my legs and arms wrapped around him. It is obvious what we're doing.

"What the fuck?" the voice says, turning around and leaving the room right away. The door slams shut.

Nate gets up in a hurry and I pull up my panties. They are wet, but there isn't much I can do about that now. I'll run to the bathroom and clean up in a moment.

"Did you know who that was?" I ask, pulling my skirt back down around my hips. It's wrinkled, but I don't think anyone will figure out why.

Nate gives me a long look, and now it's time for him to blush. I don't think I've ever seen him blush before.

"It's… Katy," he finally admits.

"Katy," I repeat incredulously. "As in, your ex, Katy?"

Nate blushes even deeper and finally nods.

"Why is she here?" I ask him.

"I have no idea," he admits, furrowing his eyebrows.

"I sure as hell didn't invite her," I snap, tugging on my clothes and feeling horribly embarrassed. A random person I could have dealt with, but the fact that his ex walked in on us makes me uncomfortable.

"I didn't either. Calm down," Nate says, giving me a sharp look. "It isn't exactly a private event."

"Yeah, but this was," I snarl motioning to the two of us in the room. I force myself to take a deep breath. "Sorry. I think I'm just a little flustered."

I don't like this. I don't like us fighting. I don't like this Katy person coming between us. I've heard how amazing she was. Layla says she thought they were going to get married at one point. Katy is supposedly gorgeous and broke Nate's heart once. I don't want her anywhere near him, especially when I'm with him.

I don't want to admit it, but I feel a little threatened by her. A woman beautiful enough to be in Hollywood who had the man I love eating out of the palm of her hand is not someone I want to see tonight. I know he says he's over her, but beautiful women are hard to forget.

"Are you gonna go talk to her?" I ask Nate, and he shrugs. "You probably should," I add.

"Fine," he says. "You're right. As usual."

He quickly pulls up his pants and kisses me softly. I can tell he's grinning, and I push him off, laughing.

"That was crazy," Nate tells me.

"Yes, it was," I agree. "Definitely not what I had planned."

"Better not get caught again," he grins.

"Better get a lock for your office," I tell him with a wink.

Nate is laughing as he leaves the room and I use the extra few minutes to find my composure. I laugh to myself and finally head back into the Perk Me Up area. If there was ever a way to show an ex who's in charge now... I've found it.

da

"Hey! Where were you?" Layla comes up to me when I come back from the bathroom.

"Err, just taking care of something," I tell her, and she gives me a doubtful look. "What's up?"

She grins. "I think that Nate is going to be able to pay off that loan after tonight."

"What?" My eyes open. "Are we really doing that much business?"

Layla grins and nods. "We've sold out of the salted caramel coffee and I have Sydney running over to the bakery to beg for more muffins. The mugs are sold out, the syrups are gone, and at least four of the paintings you hung have sold."

I stare at her. "I'll make more caramel…"

"You can't." Layla grins even wider. "We ran out of

sugar. That's how much we've sold. We can't make more caramel because we're out of freaking sugar."

My mind tries to do the mental math of just how much coffee this means we've sold tonight and I can't seem to make the numbers work. It's a lot.

"Nate is going to be so excited," I tell her.

"I know! I don't know how much he owes, but it will be really good to not have Frank breathing down his neck." Layla glances around the room. "Thank heaven he left."

"Frank was here?" I ask, looking around as if I'd recognize him. "What does he look like?"

"Handsome in a creepy way. He looks nice and charming at first, but the longer you're around him the more he twists into something not so pleasant." She shivers. "He was looking at our smoke detectors. I wonder if he was afraid his sulfur hellfire scent was going to set them off."

"You make him sound like some sort of Halloween monster," I say with a laugh.

"Oh, he's definitely as scary as one. I can't believe Nate went to him for money." Layla shakes her head. "He's wanted this building for as long as I can remember. I think he really thought he was going to get it."

"Not anymore," I tell her.

She grins. "Yup. Not anymore."

Sydney comes running up, interrupting our conversation about Frank the loan shark.

"Have you seen Audrey?" she asks, looking harried. "I can't find her."

"You lost her?" Layla asks, hands going to hips.

Sydney glares at her. "Yes. Because you told me to get

more muffins. Which I did get. I cleaned out the bakery, but I still don't think it's going to be enough. The stuff I got is nearly gone. At least the party is almost over."

"Why is Sydney watching Audrey?" I ask, looking back and forth between the two of them.

"Well, you missed a bit of drama," Layla explains.

"What happened?" I ask worriedly.

"Audrey and her boyfriend broke up right as the first band was setting up," Layla tells me. "It was all rather public. And embarrassing. There was yelling and he basically said she wasn't good in bed. She accused him of it being his fault because he's too small."

"Ouch," I say with a wince. "That's not going to end well."

"Yeah. It was brutal," Layla agrees. "But Audrey's really upset. She disappeared through the back exit, and she doesn't want to talk to anyone. Sydney was supposed to keep an eye on her."

"But instead I got muffins," Sydney replies, rolling her eyes.

"Alright, let me go talk to her," I say right away.

After all, Audrey's one of my oldest friends, and I love her dearly. I'd do anything for her, and making sure she's okay is the least I can do.

"Are you okay taking care of things here?" I ask Layla and Sydney.

Layla nods, saying, "Yup. As long as they don't riot over the lack of salted caramel."

I give her a quick hug and then quietly make my way over to the back exit. I push the heavy door open and walk into the small alley behind Perk Me Up.

No Audrey in sight.

I see something else, though.

Nathaniel and his ex, Katy, are standing a little to the side, and Nate has his hand on Katy's shoulder. They're standing close together, too close for comfort. Then Katy leans over and kisses Nate, right on the mouth.

I can only stare at them, feeling dumbfounded.

Time freezes.

On the outside, they make the perfect couple. They're both good looking, and Katy's definitely gorgeous. She looks like an old Hollywood star, and I'm just some silly girl from a high school comedy.

I remember Layla mentioning Katy. She didn't mention how beautiful and perfect she was for Nate. I don't remember her telling me how he looks so right with her. How she's much closer to his age.

They're both successful, both have aspirations, both have ideas and goals. Me? I'm just a student with an Instagram account.

How could I be a good match for anyone?

Even my own family didn't want me.

And are you ready for his life? He is not going to be an easy man to live with. He will not be able to change his habits easily. Are you really worthy of him?

My mother had warned me of this. Damn her, she had warned me and I hadn't listened.

Besides, Nate doesn't need me anymore. The shop is doing well. After tonight, he'll be able to pay off the loans. He can go back to the way things were before.

I turn around and leave the alley before I can see more. I don't even want to know whether Nate will push Katy away or pull her closer. Seeing them together is all I needed to make my decision.

I shouldn't be with him. I'm not good enough.I don't hold any illusions that I'm anything special. I am just a kid with a stupid camera. He deserves to be with someone better than me.

I don't let the tears fall until I've disappeared from Perk Me Up and headed back to my apartment. Thank fuck I haven't handed over the keys to my landlord yet.

Once I'm back at my place, I sit down at my tiny dining table, my whole body shaking. I suddenly remember I probably won't see Rocky again if I quit Perk Me Up and leave Nate.

And that thought is what finally sends me over the edge, the image of the cute, fluffy pup making the tears finally fall.

I break down the way every woman does - by myself, and with a bottle of whiskey.

ate

Once Katy and I have finished outside, I head back into Perk Me Up and immediately look around to try and find Ada. She's nowhere to be seen, so I go talk to Layla instead. She looks a little frazzled once I reach her, nervously biting her bottom lip.

"Nate, there you are," Layla says, hurrying over to me.

"What's up?" I ask her. "Where's Ada? And Audrey, for that matter?"

"I have no idea," she says. She shrugs and looks ready to burst into tears.

"Is everything alright?" I ask her in a hushed tone, and she runs her fingers through her hair in a gesture that usually means she is annoyed.

"And that has been everything for tonight, ladies and gents," Jacob finishes off on the stage, wearing a big grin.

"Thank you all for coming tonight, and making the night a big success. I'm pleased to announce we've raised enough money to send a hefty donation to the animal shelter! Feel free to add to the cash donation jar and save some puppies!"

Everyone whoops and cheers as he gets off the stage, and I lose Layla in the crowd of faces. Everyone's congratulating me, shaking my hand and wishing me good luck, and I'm busy returning smiles, good wishes and happy thoughts. It isn't until an hour later that the space has finally emptied out a little.

I say goodbye to all the people that made it tonight, including some regulars and a few people I hope will become regulars in the near future.

Once everyone files out of the cafe, I realize it's only me, Jacob and Layla. Where the hell is everyone else? I'm desperate to get Ada back in bed so I can fuck her till morning.

"Layla," I call my friend over. "What's going on? Where'd everyone else go?" I ask.

"I've no idea." She looks panicked as hell, like she's about to start pulling her hair out. "There was this whole drama with Audrey and her boyfriend," she explains to me. "And then when I told Ada, she went to fix everything, but she's disappeared now as well…"

"Wait a second, slow down a little," I tell her, hoping I can calm her down a bit so we can talk about this until it makes sense to me. "What kind of drama with Audrey?" I ask her.

"Audrey and her boyfriend had a pretty public breakup. It was embarrassing for both of them," she explains. "I was really worried about Audrey."

I pull her into a hug and she leans into me like she's absolutely exhausted. I give Jacob a confused look over her shoulder, and he mouths an I-have-no-idea at me before continuing to clean up the counter.

"Okay, and where did Audrey go?" I ask Layla once I feel she's calmed down a bit.

"She went outside," she sniffs.

"And how does Ada fit into the whole story?" I ask next.

"I told her Audrey went out through the back exit, and I asked her to go check up on her." Layla motions toward the back with her chin.

"The back exit…" It suddenly dawns on me.

Katy and I were in the alley behind Perk Me Up. And if Ada went back there, she might've…

"Fuck," I mutter to myself. "When, Layla? When did all of this happen?"

"I guess right before you came back here," she shrugs.

"Fuck," I curse out loud this time, and she gives me a surprised look. "This is bad."

"What? How?" Layla wants to know.

I'm already grabbing my jacket and heading outside.

"I'll explain everything later," I tell her. "I need to find Ada and explain. She didn't see what she thought she did."

"But don't you want to know how much money we made? It's over five–"

I shut the front door before she manages to finish her sentence.

I race to Ada's apartment. I'm breathing hard, trying to

catch my breath as I ring her doorbell like a madman. I look up into the building, and all the lights are off. I'm still hoping, though. Maybe she's there, sitting in the dark, drinking something strong. That's what I imagine her doing, anyway.

"Ada," I call out to the window. "Ada, open up, please."

No sign of her. No sign of anything, really.

I curse, running my fingers through my hair. This can't be happening. I can't have fucked up again. Not after all the mistakes I've already made.

"Ada, please," I beg her, raising my voice slightly.

It's getting pretty late, but at this point I don't give a fuck whether I'm disturbing anybody. I need to talk to Ada, first and foremost. I need to make things right between us.

As soon as Layla told me she went into the back alley, I knew she must've walked right into Katy and me.

I assume she saw Katy kiss me, which pisses me off, because I didn't want that kiss to happen. In fact, when Katy kissed me, I'd just been telling her we don't belong together.

And we really fucking don't.

Even if I'm only realizing that now.

Katy never wanted me. She only ever cared about her career.

I don't think she ever really loved me. Now that we'd been broken up for a good while though, she understood how lonely life could be, and she didn't like it. I know Katy, even though we're not together anymore. I know her like the back of my hand, and I know she craves attention. And when she realized my affection had moved to someone else, she got jealous.

So she came to me, asking me to come back to her.

And I said no.

She could shout she wanted me from the mountain-tops, and I wouldn't go back to her. We were over. We'd been over for a long time, even though I was hung up on her for a long time after we actually broke up. I told her as much in that back alley, and after I pushed her away when she tried to kiss me, she finally seemed to understand.

I swear to God, if Katy ruined this for me, I will 1-star her first movie.

"Ada!" I shout at the top of my lungs this time.

Still not a sign from her. Not a peep, not a peek.

"Ada, please. It's not what you think it is," I say lamely. I sound stupid even to myself. This is what everyone who gets caught cheating says. "Just let me explain, please. I swear it was nothing."

I sound like a bad textbook.

Instead of Ada appearing at her window or opening the door, a woman pokes her head out a different window.

"What the frick are you doing?" she shouts at me.

"I'm…" I start, sighing in frustration. "I'm just trying to get my girlfriend, Ada, to come and talk to me," I say.

"Ain't no Ada here," she grumbles.

"Ada Fucking Jones. Ada, I'm down here. Ada!" I shout, hoping she will just give me a chance to explain.

"Don't curse, young man," the older woman warns me. "I will call the cops if you don't leave right now."

"No, you don't get it," I say desperately. "I need to talk to her. I need to make things right."

She shakes her head at me dismissively.

"Don't give a damn," she tells me. "It's after midnight, you need to go home."

"But…" I start.

"Shoo!" she yells like I'm some sort of stray dog.

I stare at her angrily, and then, at the top of my voice, yell Ada's name again.

The woman mutters something and disappears back inside the building. Thank heaven for that, I didn't like her very much.

I'm about to start shouting Ada's name once again when something cold envelops me. I'm so dumbfounded for a moment I don't even realize what's happened. Not until the woman from before chuckles and I look up, ice cold water dripping down my chin.

"You needed a cold shower," she shrugs at me, then shuts her window, taking her goddamned bucket with her.

I curse, sputtering and spitting.

She just dumped a bucket of ice cold water on top of me. I'm soaked, my clothes, my hair, everything dripping with the water she just poured out of her window.

Fucking madwoman.

"Ada," I call out once more lamely, when a gust of wind chills me to the bone. "I'll be back, Ada."

I huddle into my jacket, even though it's soaked through.

I think that this night can't get any more worse when a phone call comes in.

"Mr. Rhodes? We're calling about your father…"

da

I hear the whole thing through my window. Several long, excruciatingly painful minutes after Nate's said goodbye, I get up from my armchair and peek out of the window.

He's gone.

There's only a big puddle of water down on the street.

I look at the empty glass on my coffee table, at the half-empty bottle of Jack beside it. He sounded like a fucking textbook back there, and I'm not buying any of it. Nate cheated on me, and I'm not forgiving him. Not now, not ever.

We don't fit together, anyway. I'm too young, he's too successful. Too many opposites. We don't belong with one another. Someone like Katy would be a much better fit.

I hate the thought so much I dig my nails into my

palms, barely noticing the sharp pain from what I'm doing.

There's a loud rap on my door, and my heart suddenly soars.

Could it be Nate? Could he be back so soon?

I make my way to the door, faster than I'd like to admit.

I open it wide despite promising myself I wanted to be strong, but there's no Nate on the other side of the door. Instead, I come face-to-face with my downstairs neighbor.

"Mrs. Reynolds?" I ask, feeling confused.

She harrumphs in response, and stares at me with her hands on her hips.

"You need to tell your lover boy to be quiet," she tells me sternly.

"Oh…" I gulp.

The last thing I need is for the old cow to get me in trouble with the landlord. Not now that I'm going to be staying here a little while longer.

"I'm sorry about that," I tell her through gritted teeth.

In truth, I just want to tell her to butt out of everyone's business.

She stares at me for a long time before chuckling.

"Determined, that one," she tells me.

"Who, Nate?" I ask, feeling surprised.

"Whatever his name is," she shakes her hand dismissively in the air. "You should hear him out. Perhaps not everything is as bleak as you've imagined it in that pretty little head of yours, eh?" she suggests.

I'm left staring dumbfounded at her retreating back.

Mrs. Reynolds, being one to bring together two lovers? Who would've thunk. Too bad I have no desire to hear Nate out whatsoever.

I shut the door behind my neighbor and decide I need to get away as fast as possible. I don't want to deal with my roommate whenever she gets home. I want someone who will understand how I'm feeling. I need to go to Audrey's place. I need to make sure she's alright anyway.

I give her a quick call, but she isn't answering, so I quickly pack a bag and decide to just head to her place. Thankfully, Nate doesn't have her address, so while he may ring my phone off the hook, he won't be able to find me.

I call in sick to work. I tell Meryiah not to expect me all week.

It's not mature. It's not smart.

But then I am apparently neither of those things. I want nothing to do with the coffee shop, Nate, or anyone to do with Nate.

"Hello?" I asked in a clipped tone when Layla calls me. I nearly didn't pick up the phone when I saw her number, but I feel like I should at least be a partial grownup at some point.

"Ada!" She nearly shatters my ear drum she shouts so loudly.

"Yeah," I reply without warmth.

"Ada, where are you?" she asks me desperately. "What's going on?"

"I'm with friends," I inform her. "Real friends, that is."

"What the hell is that supposed to mean?" she asks me angrily, and I shrug even though she can't see me.

"It means you probably knew about Katy and Nate all along," I spit out. All the bitterness and cruelty in me wells up and overflows. "You were probably hiding them, covering for Nate when you needed to. You knew how he felt about her."

"You have no idea how hurtful that is, Ada," she tells me softly.

"I don't care," I reply, even though my heart is breaking in half.

Not just for Nate and the pup, but for Layla as well. We've grown so close and I really love her. I am just so hurt that I want to lash out at everyone who could possibly have any responsibility. I hurt, so I want to make others hurt with me.

"But Ada, you've got it all twisted," she says, her voice shaking.

"Oh yeah?" I ask with a snort. "So Katy and Nate didn't kiss in that back alley?"

Only silence follows.

"I thought so," I reply with a sigh.

"Ada, wait..."

But I've already disconnected the call. After that, I block her number right along with Nate's.

After a couple days have passed, my head clears up a little, and now I'm stuck in the black hole of doubting myself.

Actually, I'm past doubting myself and full on hating

what I've done. I let bitterness and fear trump love. Nate deserved a chance to explain. Layla didn't do anything wrong.

I am a total bitch. I screwed up.

If I wanted to show my age and inexperience, this was a blue-ribbon winning exhibit of how not mature I can be.

I don't deserve Nate. There's no fixing this now. I pushed him far away enough to make sure he'd never come back, and now I have to reap what I sowed.

I even consider calling my mother and telling her she was right. I consider going back to my mother's dominion and just letting her dictate my life. I would make a lot fewer stupid mistakes that way.

But my art would suffer. I wouldn't be me anymore. Even if I'm young and stupid, I have value. I have worth. I have a gift for pictures and words to make people feel things when they see what I have created, and I am not going to give that up.

So I dive into my project. Since I called in sick, that means I have a bunch of extra time to work on it, making sure that it is what I want it to be, what I saw in my head the first time I came up with the idea.

It is a story about love.

I edit all my footage. I make it absolutely perfect.

After I submit it to my professor, I feel a sense of letting go. It's not exactly peace, but it is something that makes the ache in my heart just a little bit better. I may be a terrible girlfriend, but at least my video will make the world a little more beautiful. I hope it balances out my karma at least a little bit.

I'm too scared to go back to my place, so I ask Jacob to

bring me some stuff from there. He's feeling conflicted, torn between new friends and old ones, and I can tell this is weighing on him pretty heavily as well.

He does bring me some stuff back though, and once he comes back with my things, he's wearing a big bright smile.

"I brought you coffee," Jacob announces. "In addition to the things you requested."

"Gimme!" I hold my hands out, motioning for the sweet beverage like a small child.

He hands over the sweet caffeine, chuckling as Audrey and I making cooing happy noises. I've missed my good coffee. I've become horribly spoiled by working at Perk Me Up and having access to amazing coffee all the time.

I now understand why Nate opened it. I'm considering opening a coffee shop myself just so I can get a good cup of coffee without having to run into someone I know.

Jacob heads for the window, pulling up the blinds. Audrey hisses on the couch, covering her face with her hand and blocking the light.

"Poison!" she hisses, and it even makes me chuckle.

We've both been permanently PJ'd up, and are now hooked on a Spanish telenovela that we've binged for the past six hours straight. I'm fairly certain we've eaten nothing but ice cream and pizza. Talk about getting over a break up.

"Are you ever going to come back to work?" Jacob asks, moving an empty ice cream carton from the couch so he can sit down. "As much as I love the extra money, the overtime is killing me."

I slouch lower in my guilt. "Do you think they'd let me?"

"You just need to talk to Nate. I promise it won't be that bad," Jacob tells me.

"Right. And lava is just some kind of hot rocks. It'll be fine."

Jacob rolls his eyes at me, and I can't say I blame him. I am being dramatic, but it's because I don't know what else to do. I've made a fool of myself and I don't know if I can go crawling back.

There's a short rap on the door. Audrey and I exchange looks. We aren't expecting anyone else today.

"I'll get it," I tell her, since my pajamas are more socially appropriate than hers.

I peek through the peephole, but I don't see anyone out on the hallway. Confused, I open the door and look around - no one there.

A noise makes me look down, though, and despite not wanting to, I can't resist a smile.

He's grown since I've last seen him, but Rocky is still the cutest puppy there is. He's wearing an enormous red bow around his neck along with a party hat on his little head, and he's wagging his tail excitedly at the sight of me.

"What are you doing here, buddy?" I ask him, leaning down to hug the dog.

It is only then that I realize Rocky couldn't have possibly knocked on the door himself, which can only mean one thing. Nate is somewhere close.

Speak of the devil.

The man himself walks from the stairway, approaching me sheepishly. He's doing that thing he always does when he's nervous, running his hands through his dark hair, which he left messy today. As I stare at him, I feel regret and pain sinking into the pit of my stomach. I want to touch him. Feel his body against mine one last time.

"What are you doing here?" I ask him tersely.

Nate stops in front of Audrey's door, and I can hear how quiet my two friends have gone behind me. We're all waiting for my reaction, and even I don't know what it's going to be.

"Can we talk?" Nate asks me softly, and I shake my head right away.

"Ada." He steps closer, his hand going to my shoulder.

I flinch when he touches me, but not because I hate it. I want his touch so badly that I'm shaking. I want to throw myself at him, to tell him that I need him and that I love him. I want to tell him that being apart has made my soul hurt.

But my pride won't let me.

"Ada Jones, you will listen to me," Nate tells me.

"Oh? You're giving me orders now?" I ask with a raised eyebrow.

"Holy shit, Ada," Nate groans. "Why do you have to be so difficult?"

"Why do you have to be so… impossible?" I ask lamely, waving my hands around angrily.

"Because you love it," Nate replies in a small voice.

"Not true," I say sharply.

"Stop looking for a reason, Ada," Nate tells me.

"A reason?"

"To leave me," he says softly, and it finally makes me shut up.

Maybe he's right. Maybe I have been trying hard to cut him off, make things easier on both of us. Maybe I really am still convinced we'd be happier apart. Once again, I wonder if my mother's words really did get into my head.

"If you'd only let me explain," he continues. "And do not send me on this wild goose chase to find you. I knew you were staying at Audrey's. Hi, by the way," he waves to my friends behind my back, and Audrey returns an awkward hello. "Thank god for Jacob.".

I look over my shoulder at my friend, and he's blushing guiltily. Great. Just fucking great. Just when I thought I could trust him, he goes and blabs to Nate.

Of course, I'd be lying if I said I wasn't a little pleased about it. It means Nate is here, and it means he still cares…

I shake my head. I can't let myself fall back into that black hole. I need to keep my head clear and deal with this problem the only way I know how - by pushing everyone away.

"Why are you here, Nate?" I ask him, despite wanting to just run away from it all.

"To make things right," he replies. I notice then that he has a backpack on. He swings it off his shoulder and unzips the bag.

He pulls out flowers.

For a moment, I wonder if he's about to propose. The scary thing is, I'm not sure I would say no.

Then he pulls out a container of soup.

I frown. "You brought me flowers and soup?"

"You called in sick," he explains. "So, flowers, chicken noodle soup, some zinc, a bottle of ginger ale, orange juice, and a bottle of vitamins."

He pulls out each item from his bag, setting them

down so that I can see the assortment of things he brought to make me feel better.

"And Rocky," Nate adds. "Because he's really missed you."

I break then. I fall to my knees, sobbing with released pain and sudden joy.

Nate understands. He is next to me in a second, wrapping his arms around me and holding me while I sob into him.

"Please know there is nothing going on between Katy and me," Nate tells me next, his eyes pleading with me to understand. "Since the day I met you, I've only wanted you. No one fucking else. Only you."

"Nate, I'm so sorry–"

He cuts me off with a kiss.

"I love you," I whisper when he pulls back from me. "I don't deserve you, but I love you."

He chuckles. "I'm the one who doesn't deserve you. Did you see the party you threw me? Also, you kept doing the social media all this time."

I blush. I did keep posting. Just because I was being awful didn't mean that I wanted Nate and Perk Me Up to suffer. So, I posted more videos and kept the marketing going.

"I have a question for you," Nate says, taking my hands in his. He looks into my eyes, holding me captive. I forget to breathe.

"Yes?" The word squeaks out of me.

"Will you move in with me?" he asks. "Rocky and I miss you. And I can't say that I'm a fan of your neighbor."

"Yes," I tell him. Behind me, Jacob and Audrey start clapping.

"You can move as soon as you help me clean up," Audrey announces. "You don't get out of cleaning that easily."

da

I go back to work with a batch of cookies just for Layla.

"I am a total bitch and I'm so sorry," I gush the moment I see her.

She's wearing lime green tights with pink polkadots, an amazing pink dress that definitely has pockets, and a black shrug sweater. Her hair is streaked with green and pink. On anyone else it would look ridiculous, but on her it's amazing. I want to take her photo so badly, but I've already asked too much of her.

She crosses her arms and glares at me.

"If we're going to be friends, I need you to promise me something."

"Anything," I reply, holding out the cookies.

She glances at the pumpkin chocolate chip cookies like she might say no, but then snatches them away from me.

"You have to give me the benefit of the doubt. Always," she tells me. "Nate can go screw himself. I don't care what he does, but you give ME a chance."

Red hot embarrassment washes over me again. I wish I could sink into the floor. I wish I could go back in time and take back what I said to her. Layla didn't deserve it. She didn't do anything wrong.

"I solemnly swear to always hear you out," I say, holding up my hand.

Layla looks me over, as if evaluating if I'm telling the truth.

"And I'm really sorry," I blurt out. "I am awful and I owe you cookies for at least a week."

She picks one of the cookies out of the plastic container and takes a bite. Her eyelids flutter a little bit.

"How did you know these were my favorite?" she asks, chewing slowly and glaring at me again.

"They're my favorite," I reply. "And you have amazing taste so I thought you might enjoy them too."

"Hmm. Flattery will get you back in my good graces," she informs me, popping the rest of the cookie back in her mouth.

"In that case, you are the smartest, most beautiful, most understanding, most awesome coworker and friend I have," I tell her.

"It's over the top, but I like it." She grins at me. "A few more weeks of groveling and I think I'll be ready to forgive you."

Which really means she forgives me now. A weight lifts from my shoulders. I hug Layla and she hugs me back. I still feel a little guilty, and I secretly promise myself that I am going to make her at least three more batches of cookies. She deserves all of them and then some.

"Go get behind the counter," Layla says, releasing me from the hug. "You can start your shift a little early."

I happily hop around behind the counter and put on my apron to start work. Customers are already coming in for the afternoon rush and I know I'll keep busy for the rest of the afternoon.

Work goes quickly and it feels good to be back. Layla and Sydney have me laughing as I wipe tables and do all the tasks that no one likes without being asked. It's the least I can do and it helps assuage my guilt at leaving them short-staffed this week.

A little after dinner, the cafe starts to quiet down. We still have dozens of students, but the hurried rush for caffeine has shifted into a more mellow buzz of activity.

"Hey, Newbie," a deep voice greets me.

I turn slowly from the register to see Nate walking toward me. He's wearing khaki slacks that look amazing on his ass and a fitted polo t-shirt with the Perk Me Up logo on the chest. I love the way his eyes light up when I turn around, as if seeing me is the best part of his day.

"Hey boss," I reply. I grin. "Or, should I say, roomie."

The smile that lights up Nate's face could power an entire city.

"I'd kiss you, but I'm pretty sure that's against the health code," he says, coming to stand next to me.

"You'll just have to do it later," I tell him with a naughty wink. "One of the perks of living with me."

He looks at me like he might decide to violate the

health code, but then takes a step back as a customer walks in.

"Ada, I didn't know you worked here," Professor Gains says, coming up to the counter. He looks exactly like what I think a professor should look like- messy hair, a beard, and patches on the elbows of his jacket.

"Good evening, Professor," I greet him. "Nate, this is my photography professor. Dr. Gains, this is the owner of Perk Me Up, Nate Rhodes."

"It's very nice to meet you," Dr. Gains replies. "I have to tell you, your new salted caramel coffee has me addicted. I think it's the only thing that's going to get me through these mid-term projects."

Nate's chest puffs out and he grins at me. "Hopefully that means you'll give Ada the best grades since she came up with the recipe."

"It's actually wonderful that I ran into you, Ada. I wanted to talk to you about your project," Dr. Gains replies, his careful gaze coming to look at me.

"Is there something wrong with it?" I ask. "I can send it in another format, and i have all the paperworks–"

"No, no, there is absolutely nothing wrong with it," Dr. Gains cuts me off. "Actually, it's the best work I've seen in years. I was hoping you'd let me enter you for a scholarship. And let me show your film at the short film festival in a few weeks."

I stare at him, my mouth hanging open.

"You want to offer a scholarship because of her project?" Nate asks. He puts his arm around me. "That's amazing!"

"Yes," Dr. Gains agrees. "And the film festival has some

prizes as well that I think she'll win. Like I said, I haven't seen a film that moved me as much as yours did in years. You have a real talent."

"You liked it?" I gasp, still in shock.

"I loved it," Dr. Gains replies. "And so did the rest of my staff. You had us all in tears. The Dean was already talking about making a donation to Alzheimer's research."

"Wait, Alzheimer's research?" Nate's arm tightens a little around my shoulders. He turns to face me. "That's what your project was on?"

I can't tell if he's angry or just surprised. I start to fiddle with my necklace, sliding the bird up and down the chain.

Dr. Gains doesn't notice the tension suddenly between us, or if he does, he is polite enough not to say anything.

"Anyway, I'll send you all the information," he says, clearing his throat. "And I'll just take an extra large salted caramel with extra whip."

I robotically slide his card and Layla makes the coffee while Nate stares at me. It feels like the cafe has gone extra quiet. There are no more customers in line after the professor, so I don't have anything to do with my hands once Dr. Gains leaves the shop with his coffee.

"Alzheimer's?" Nate repeats.

I swallow hard.

"Let me show you the video," I say quickly. I look around the shop and see that it's not too busy. "We can watch it on my laptop over here."

I grab my laptop and Nate follows me out from behind the counter. Layla and Sydney aren't far behind.

I set it up on a table in the corner, and Nate takes the

seat in front of it. I still can't tell if he's angry or just confused. It doesn't matter, though, my heart is pounding in my chest. I had planned on showing him the video, but not quite like this.

But it's time for Nate to meet his father again.

da

We all stare at the screen silently.

I press play.

Nathaniel's father comes alive on the screen, laughing silently as my voice tells everyone the date of that particular day of filming.

"He was a horribly disobedient child," Ada's father says in a shaky voice. "He'd scream all day as a baby, and he was stubborn as heck when he got older, but I loved him so much. The first moment I held him in my arms, I knew he was going to change my life."

I reach for Nate, resting my hand on his shoulder. He's watching motionlessly, without saying a single word.

His father continues on the screen.

"I've always loved him. I always will. I sometimes forget… things." He swallows hard, tears pooling in his eyes. "I do stupid things. I think he'd prefer it if I were gone."

Nate's shoulder tightens under my hand.

"But I never go through with it, because even if I... even if I don't know him sometimes, I always feel the love for him. Here."

The man on his screen puts a hand on his chest.

"Right here. I love my son, even if I can't always say it."

The scene changes to leaves changing colors, and my voice says another date, only a day later.

Nate's father comes into focus, standing amidst the falling leaves.

"Hello," he says pleasantly. "Have we met?"

I can hear Layla sniffle softly behind me.

I say another date in the movie. A few days later.

"That day at the beach was my favorite," Nate's father tells me. "We built a sandcastle, and the sea washed it away an hour later, when the high waters came. Nathaniel was devastated."

"I remember that day," Nate says softly. "I was so upset."

"I took him for a walk along the shore. I told him things are ever changing, from something as simple as a sandcastle to something as complicated as feelings."

The man on the screen swallows hard.

"I told him there is one thing that will never change. I will always love him, even when my body and mind are gone. I will always be his father. And he will always carry me in his heart."

I feel Nate take a shuddering breath beneath my hand and I give him a gentle squeeze of reassurance.

"He told me I was silly," Nate's father says with a laugh.

"Told me I may be ancient - I was thirty at the time - but that I seemed pretty wise."

We all laugh in the now quiet room.

"He promised me he wouldn't forget though. Wouldn't forget what I told him, and wouldn't forget the memory of his Dad."

"I haven't," Nate says quietly.

The movie keeps rolling and we all watch in silence.

There are longer sequences of Nate's father talking about his son. Shorter ones of him looking lonely, confused. Not remembering. Perking up when he sees me approaching with the camera. Perking up every time he gets a visitor.

Smiling.

Crying.

Regret.

Hope.

It's all in there, on the screen.

It's time for the last frame.

Nate's father is sitting in the garden, leaves falling down around him, autumn finally happening in full force. Suddenly, he gets up, and kicks at the pile of fallen leaves on the ground like a small child about to jump in. He looks at the camera, and he laughs. A pure, happy sound, a sound that reminds me of happy days, filled with the scent of coffee, the taste of caramel, and filled with hope.

The frame fades to black, and soft music begins to play, fading out the story.

We all sit there and contemplate what we've just seen. I think I outdid myself with the film, and more than that, it means so much to me. Those hours, those days I spent with Nate's father were special to me.

It was all for Nate.

I wanted to show him the film. Wanted to show him that, while we'll always be his family, his father still needs him. Loves him. He's still there.

Nate turns around in the chair slowly until we're face to face.

"I…" he begins, his voice breaking.

I hold my necklace in my hand, not playing with it, but just holding it close to me. "He loves you."

"I didn't know," he admits, his eyes darting back to the screen.

"He loves you," I tell him. "Even if he can't remember… He feels the love. He feels you, like a missing piece of his heart."

Nate nods, tears rolling down his cheeks.

The final frame of my film is a still image of Mr. Rhodes standing in the leaves, the sunlight on his face. His eyes are closed as he looks toward the sky, but he looks content and happy.

"How did you do this?" he asks, reaching for the screen. His finger traces the edge of his father's face with a gentle stroke.

"Remember how I asked you to sign the paperwork for me to visit?" I ask. "And then the forms for me to take pictures?"

Nate nods. "I didn't think you were going to get anything usable."

"I went on my days off," I continue. "The nurses would help me and let me know what kind of day he was having and what questions to ask to get him to start talking."

"How long?" Nate asks, his eyes still glued to his father's face. "How long have you been doing this?"

"About a month."

A small smile flits across his lips. "Did you know that he didn't try to run at all this month?" Nate finally looks at me. "No escape attempts this month. He's been a model citizen. The nurses were so pleased to tell me."

I raise my eyebrows.

"I actually got a call the other day. Someone made an anonymous complaint about him, saying that they found him in their house and he'd run off." Nate shakes his head. "But the complaint was dismissed. He hasn't eloped in over a month. A month that you've been visiting him."

"Someone said he'd broken into their house?" I ask, shocked.

"Yes, but that he'd run off and must have gotten back into the facility. It has happened before, at a different facility," Nate replies. "However, whoever made the complaint must have been confused. Not a single camera has him attempting to leave. Usually there are several attempts a week, but not this month."

"And the complaint?" I ask, anxiety tugging at my chest.

"It was dropped. Without any escape attempts this month, it was clear it couldn't have been him." He smiles at me. "The nurses say he's less aggressive and anxious. HIs memory isn't any better, but he's having more good days than bad."

"I'm glad he's doing better," I tell him.

He takes my hands, our eyes connecting. "Now that I know you've been visiting, I think it's you."

"I just went and asked him questions." I shrug, feeling a blush cross my face. "I didn't do anything special."

"No, you treated him like a person," Nate tells me.

"You gave him his humanity again. You gave him this." He points to the laptop. "It's easy to forget that there is a person in there sometimes. That they are just as scared and frightened of what is happening to them as we are."

I don't know what to say. Warmth rushes through me as Nate takes me in his arms and hugs me.

"We should go visit him," I say when he releases me.

"I'd love that," Nate agrees.

CHAPTER 39

 ate

We stay at the nursing home until the nurses kick us out. My father laughed, actually laughed, at a pun Ada made. He didn't remember who we were, but he enjoyed our company and was sad when the nurses told us to leave.

It was a wonderful evening and my heart feels lighter than it has in months. I didn't realize how much guilt, sorrow, and grief I was carrying around with me over my father. I still am, to be honest, but at least I don't feel overwhelmed by it.

I read that dementia is constantly having to say goodbye. Goodbye to the person you love, goodbye to the life they had, goodbye to the relationship you once knew. The worst part is that sometimes, there will be moments where the goodbye stops and then you have to start all over again.

I look over at Ada as we drive home, trying to imprint the way she looks right now in my memory so I will never forget her. I'm still terrified that my father's genes will haunt me, and thus her, but she's shown more grace and compassion than I could ever hope to have.

"Ada…"

She looks over at me and smiles. She's tired, but in the darkness is beautiful and lovely. She is more lovely than the thin crescent moon hanging low in the night sky. It won't be long before winter comes.

"I love you, Nate." She reaches her hand through the darkness and squeezes my knee. Her hand is warm even through the fabric of my pants. "Actually, I was thinking of something."

"Yes?" My heart skips a beat, but then settles when I remember that she loves me.

"We need a peppermint mocha coffee." Her eyes go distant as she looks out the front of the car at the dark road in front of us. "Or maybe a gingerbread latte. I unfortunately don't have a secret family recipe for either of those, but we should come up with one."

A happy, contented warmth fills me. She's planning for the future. Our future.

"I think we should do both," I agree. "But you should come up with the recipe. My caramel was… not good."

Her laugh is light and sweet as we pull into the parking structure for my building. It's dark out tonight, the crescent moon barely giving any light. The trees here are bare now, the brightly colored leaves still scattered through the parking lots and dancing with every gust of wind.

Ada steps out of the car and shivers, pulling her sweater tighter around her.

"Let's get you inside," I tell her. "You start a fire and I'll give Rocky a bathroom break."

She agrees and quickly hurries inside. Rocky is dancing and whining at the door, ready to be let out. I think he's grown in just the time we were gone, his legs getting long and lanky even though his paws are still huge and fluffy.

"Hey buddy," I say, ruffling the soft fur on his head. "You ready?"

He yips a bark and I clip the leash to his collar and head back downstairs. Rocky practically pulls me to the back alley so that he can run around the small space smelling everything before deciding to use his favorite potty spot.

We wander around the back alley for a few minutes, making sure that he has plenty of time to empty his bladder for the evening. A cold wind is blowing through and I can't wait to get back inside.

"Come on, Rocky," I say after a while. "I want to go back in."

But Rocky refuses, pulling on the leash and trying to go to the far end of the small back space.

"There is nothing over there," I tell him. "All the bunnies are asleep."

But, still he pulls.

I sigh. "Ada is waiting inside with dinner…"

At the mention of the word dinner, his fluffy ears perk up and he stops pulling. He looks at the far fence, wags his tail twice and then bounds back to be with me. I shake my head. I knew mentioning food and Ada would have him coming back inside.

Upstairs, Ada has a crackling fire going that makes the room feel warm and comforting. She already has a bowl of food out for Rocky, which he dives into with gusto.

Ada and I snuggle on the couch, talking softly about ideas for the coffee shop and watching the small fire burn down to coals.

"What if we opened a second location?" Ada asks. "I know this building was your fathers and is prime real estate, but what about something on the opposite side of campus?"

I think. "There's an old restaurant building that's been for sale for ages over on the north side. It probably wouldn't be too hard to upgrade it. Especially now that I don't have that loan anymore."

Ada sits straight up. "Wait, you paid it off?"

I grin at her. "This morning. I won't be taking a paycheck this week, but I think being out from under Frank's thumb is worth it."

She beams at me. "I'm so proud of you."

"You're the one that made it possible," I tell her, wrapping her up in my arms. She smells like caramel and coffee and everything good in the world. "I couldn't have done it without you."

"And don't you forget it," she mumbles into my shoulder, holding on to me. "But, I'm still really glad you don't have that hanging over you any more."

"You and me both. I do have to say that I thought Frank was going to have a heart attack." I shake my head. Frank's face would forever stay in my mind. He'd nearly turned purple when I'd handed him that check. "He's wanted this building for years. I really thought he might get it. I think he did too."

"But it's staying yours," she tells me.

I nod. "Now I can start making upgrades. You wait, this place is going to be amazing again. It'll be like when I was a kid. We'll upgrade everything and make it all top of the line again."

She smiles sleepily. "I can imagine. It'll be great."

"You need to go to bed," I tell her. She yawns in response. "We'll dream more about new locations and revamping this one tomorrow."

"I want a new kitchen," she mumbles, standing up from the coach. "Layla does too. The one we have now is too small."

"Yes, mistress," I reply. "A new kitchen."

She sticks her tongue out at me but then yawns again.

We both change into pajamas and climb into bed. Rocky takes a spot by our feet where he's close enough to touch us, but less likely to be kicked when we move. Ada snuggles into me, the little spoon to my bigger one. I breathe in the scent of her, feeling my body relax around her. It feels so right to have her in my arms. I love the way her body goes loose and limp as sleep takes her.

And I follow her to dreamland.

da

I keep dreaming about firefighters. They are burly and sexy, but I don't want them to kiss me. I just want Nate. It's a very strange dream.

I wake up, smelling smoke.

I must have not set the fire up right, I think to myself. It's smoking up the house even though we made sure it was burned out when we went to bed. I figure that's why I was dreaming about firefighters.

Rocky is barking.

"Rocky, it's just some smoke from the fireplace," I groan, trying to pull a pillow up over my head. "It's fine."

But the damn dog won't stop. His yips come loud and fast, and he bites at the blanket, growling as he tries to pull it off of us.

Finally, I sit up, ready to yell at him but when I do I see just how smokey the room is.

And the fact that I can see without turning on a light. An orange light is flickering under the door, making strange shadows on the walls.

Panic settles into my bones as I realize that the place is on fire.

"Nate, wake up," I shout, shaking the sleeping man next to me.

"It's fine," he mumbles. "Sometimes the fireplace backs up. It'll be fine."

"It's not fine," I scream, shaking him harder. "The house is on fire!"

That wakes him up. He sits up, rubbing his eyes as he looks around.

"Why aren't the smoke detectors going off?" he asks. "They should be going off."

"It doesn't matter," I tell him, throwing off the covers of the bed and grabbing a pair of shoes. The orange light on the other side of the door is brighter and I swear the room is getting hot. The scent of acrid smoke, so different from the pleasant wood fire, fills my nose. This smell is bitter and full of hate.

It smells like death coming.

Rocky keeps barking at us, telling us that we need to get going.

Nate reaches for the doorknob but hisses, pulling his hand into his chest.

"It's burning hot," he tells me. His eyes are wide with fear now.

"The window," we both say at the same time. I reach it first.

The bedroom window looks out over the front of the coffee shop. I push the heavy curtains to the sides, suddenly hating them. The window sticks as I try to lift the old glass pane up. The windows are ancient and heavy and I'm fairly sure they have been painted over several times. I can't get them open.

Nate doesn't hesitate. He comes up behind me, and has me move to the side. He throws a lamp at the window, shattering the night with the sound of breaking glass. Fresh air pours into the bedroom and I gasp, suddenly coughing and feeling lightheaded.

Nate wraps his arm up in a bedsheet and clears the broken glass from the frame. He helps me climb up and for a moment, I am terrified.

The window is on the second story. There is nothing to climb on and only cement and street below me to break my fall. A jump from this height will only break bones if I'm lucky. I glance back at the bedroom door, debating if trying to get through the flames might be the better option.

"There's a fire escape ladder," Nate informs me, reaching under the window and pulling a metal ladder free. It looks like it's made of tin foil and will break any moment, but it is far better than jumping.

"What about Rocky?" I ask.

"I've got him," Nate assures me. "Just get down."

Still, the smoke alarms don't go off. There is only the sound of hungry flames, the crackle of wood lighting, and the pop and hiss of things in the kitchen burning.

It's getting hotter for sure now. Flames lick at the edges of the bedroom door and Rocky is frantic. I climb through the broken window, trying not to catch my pjs on the broken glass. The ladder is rickety as hell and my hands are slippery on the metal. It's just metal chains with thin strips of metal at regular intervals all the way down. With each step down, the ladder swings, but the steps don't give way.

I step out on the concrete with shaking legs and look up.

Nate has Rocky stuffed in a backpack. He is zipped in so that only his head is sticking out, and I'm suddenly glad that he's still just a small puppy. I don't know if Nate had a backpack big enough for a full grown dog. Rocky looks absolutely furious about this arrangement and he whines pitifully as Nate makes his way down the ladder and to the street.

I hug him, finding that he's shaking just as much as I am.

"Dad always had a thing for fire safety," Nate says, his hand still on the metal fire ladder. "I'm really glad he saved us tonight."

The bedroom suddenly explodes with fire and light. Nate moves to shield me with his body as flames rush out the window, lunging for the fresh air. The heat singes my skin and makes my throat dry.

"We have to get across the street," he shouts, pulling me away from the building.

Fire engines start to arrive. There is smoke and chaos, but Nate and I just stand and watch as the building goes up in orange and yellow flames. Everything moves in slow motion and then in hyper speed, as if someone were playing with the pause and fast forward buttons on a remote.

Nate lets Rocky out of the backpack, keeping him on a

short leash. He doesn't have to try too hard. Rocky is cowering beneath our feet, unwilling to let us move from where he can touch us.

"Is there anyone else in the building?" a fireman asks Nate. It's hard to understand him with all the noise of the fire, the hoses, the firetrucks, Rocky barking, and everyone shouting.

"No. It was just us in this building," Nate replies. "The building next door should be unoccupied. They're just offices, no one is living in them."

"Good. Because we can't get in there," the fireman says. He stops and looks at the building. "I've never seen a building go up so quickly. You are lucky to be alive."

Nate puts an arm around my shoulder, pulling me into him. He smells like acrid smoke, but I don't care. He's solid and strong and safe.

The flames spread to the coffee shop. Through the plate glass windows, I can see the chairs melting. My art on the walls catches quickly and is gone up in flames in seconds. The smell of burnt coffee and melting plastic permeates the air.

We watch as the building, the building that held all our hopes and dreams, the place that brought us together, that made us friends and family, burns. The coffee shop and our home is gone.

CHAPTER 41

Ada

"The fire is almost out," a firefighter informs us. His jacket is covered with smoke and ash. "It shouldn't have gone up that quickly. We found some containers of gasoline in the back alley. Do you keep anything stored back there?"

"Gas?" Nate repeats. "We don't have anything like that back there."

"Then it was probably arson," the firefighter replies. "The police will look into it."

I sit with my back against the bakery, my arms wrapped protectively around Rocky. I don't want to watch my home and place of employment burn, but I can't look away. I can only imagine how Nate feels watching it crumble to ash.

Arson. I try to think of who could do this.

An uncomfortable idea comes to me that it might have been my mother. I have no doubt that she was the "anonymous" person who supposedly found Mr. Rhodes in her house and was trying to get him kicked out of the facility, but this feels worse.

Would my own mother light the house I am sleeping in on fire to get me to leave?

I want to say no, but a small part of me wonders.

"Thank you," Nate says to the firefighter, looking like he might fall over in a stiff wind. Every line of him looks exhausted. His face is older and more drawn than I've ever seen. There is a giant streak of ash across his left cheek and soot makes his hair gray.

"Do you have a place to go?" the firefighter asks.

"They're coming with me," a female voice informs him. I look over to see Layla stomping up the street. Two police officers are following her looking frustrated and confused.

She's wearing rainbow striped pajamas, fluffy bunny slippers, and a fierce look on her face.

"Layla!" I stand up and run to her, throwing my arms around her. She hugs me back hard.

"I started getting calls an hour ago about the cafe being on fire," she explains. "These gentlemen..." she turns and glares at the two police men following her, "wouldn't let me pass."

"It's a safety..." the first one starts to say and then stops when she levels a glare at him that makes me feel bad for him.

"Anyway, you two are coming with me. My car is parked around the block. They aren't letting anyone down the street," she tells us. She loops her elbow with mine and starts leading us down the block.

The farther we get from the fire, the more people I see. The police have blocked off the entirety of Main Street and it has created a lot of people watching. I see a news truck and enough flashing lights to make my head hurt.

Layla puts us in her car and drives us away from all of it.

∾

The fire was set by Frank.

The police found gasoline all around the property as well as that all our smoke detectors had been tampered with.

They say that we were lucky to escape with our lives.

I am glad that it wasn't my fire in the fireplace that started it.

I am glad that it wasn't my mother who lit the match.

But I am heartbroken at our loss. At Nate's loss.

He has lost everything we worked so hard to achieve. He had a thriving business, a home, and the world was finally coming together for him. This fire took all of it.

"Why so sad?" he asks me, joining me at Layla's tiny kitchen table for breakfast. We're wearing new pajamas bought at the store. They have the uncomfortable feeling that they need to be washed a few more times to make them soft.

We won't be able to stay here long. Nate is sleeping on the floor while insisting I take the futon couch. I'm not sure that it's actually that much more comfortable.

I appreciate that Layla has put us up for a few days, but her apartment is made for barely one person. The three of us are cramped and uncomfortable. I wish I still had my little apartment, but it's already been rented out to a different student.

"Just…" I sigh. "I'm so sorry about this, Nate. About everything."

He frowns. "What? Why?"

"Because you just lost everything," I explain.

He smiles, taking my hands in his.

"I lost things," he tells me. "But I didn't lose everything. I still have Rocky. I still have you. That's all I need."

"That's sweet, but you worked so hard on your business. Your home," I reply.

He shrugs. "That's why I have insurance. Those are just things. You are what's important."

"But–"

"No buts, Newbie," he says. He reaches into his pajama pants pocket, his hand tightening on something. "I wanted to wait, but now it feels right."

"What do you mean?" I ask, but he's already kneeling on the linoleum floor in front of me.

"This was my mother's ring. My father told me that I would know when the right woman came along for me to give it to," he says, pulling out a small black velvet box from his pocket. "I've known for a while now that it was you, Ada."

My brain goes completely blank as I stare at him. My heart is pounding and I feel like I'm floating.

"I had a big event planned," he continues. "A fancy dinner, all our friends at the cafe…" He looks up at me and shrugs ruefully. "But this is better."

"This is better?" I ask, looking around Layla's tiny kitchen. There are cereal bowls stacked in the sink. Rocky is snoring beneath the table. I'm wearing cheap pajamas and Nate is proposing with Froot Loops scattered on the table.

He grins. "It's better because I know without a shadow of a doubt that you are the one I want in my life. There is no doubt in my mind that I want to spend the rest of my life with you. All I thought about with those flames coming after us was that I hadn't had enough time with you yet."

My heart starts to melt.

"So, I am asking you to marry me in the least romantic place in the world, not because I lust for you or because I want anything from you," he continues. "I'm asking you to marry me because I love you and I can't wait another minute to ask you to join me. I love you in every place of this world."

He opens the box, showing me the ring.

It's delicate and beautiful with a blue sapphire set in the center of the room that sparkles.

"So, Ada Jones, will you make me the happiest man in the world and marry me?"

I don't have to think about it. I fall to the floor beside him, wrapping my arms around his neck and whispering yes.

Nate proposes to me again after a week. This time, he does it in a fancy restaurant with all our friends. The second time I have on a pretty dress and my hair and nails look perfect for pictures. Layla pretends like she didn't know about the first one and swoons over both of us. Sydney, Jacob, Meryiah, and all the staff cheer.

I like that he included our friends. I like that we have a

traditional proposal with champagne and cheers, but also that I had one that was just the two of us.

The days after the fire should have been the worst of our lives, but they weren't because we had each other.

We found a small house to rent just outside of town. It has a backyard for Rocky to run around in, but it's still walking distance to school.

We're waiting to have the wedding until the cafe is rebuilt. We'll have it there. The insurance money is more than enough to make the cafe into everything we want it to be. Plus, there should be enough left over for us to start a second location.

My mother is still unhappy. I don't think she will ever be pleased with my choices, but she is not the one who has to live with them. My father has decided to come to my wedding, with or without her.

I love my choices. I am happy.

I love Nathan. I will always chose him. I will always want to find his warmth in the cool of the evening. I will always find my way back to him. I don't want to find anyone else.

Fall is almost over. There are no more leaves on the trees, the pumpkins have all been picked, and the sparkling lights of Christmas and the promise of snow hangs heavy in the air. Yet, I will always love the season of fall.

Fall is the season of love.

Escape With Me: A Midlife Love Story

"I gave it all up to be happy. I'd give it all up again for you."

They say life begins after 40, but Cassie ain't feelin' it. Divorced and feeling trapped by her job, she wants to let loose for her friend's tropical beach wedding. She decides to let her hair down and get a little unpredictable. That's when she meets a handsome bartender, Wyatt.

Despite a few grey hairs, Wyatt's the liveliest man that Cassie has ever met. She knows that there's got to be more to his life story than just being a bartender, but this is just supposed to be a vacation fling. And after sunny days spent breaking all the rules on the beach together, Cassie realizes that nobody has ever listened to her the way that Wyatt does.

His carefree life is enviable, his kisses are intoxicating, and she can almost imagine a life with him. But all vacations come to an end. And when Cassie invites him to visit her hometown, Wyatt reveals that he can never go back. Not to her town. Not to America. Not to civilization.

Cassie leaves, confused and heartbroken, wondering just who she got herself involved with. Suddenly, her predictable life gets turned upside down when she sees her picture splashed across the Internet. And when the tabloids come looking for the mature woman who found the lost billionaire, she has no idea what to do...

...until he comes back.

Escape With Me: A Midlife Love Story

ABOUT THE AUTHOR

New York Times and USA Today Bestseller Krista Lakes is a thirtysomething who recently rediscovered her passion for writing. She is living happily ever after with her Prince Charming. Her first kid just started preschool and she is happy to welcome her second child into her life, continuing her "Happily Ever After"!

Thank you for supporting an indie author. Anything you can do, whether it be writing a review, or even simply telling a fellow reader that you enjoyed this, helps me out immensely. Thanks!

Krista would love to hear from you! Please contact her at Krista.Lakes@gmail.com or friend her on Facebook!

Further reading:

Bad Boys and Babies
    Family Doctor's Baby
    The Billionaire's Baby Arrangement
    Crime Boss Baby

Kinds of Love
    A Forever Kind of Love
    A Wonderful Kind of Love

An Endless Kind of Love

Billionaires and Brides
Yours Completely: A Cinderella Love Story
Yours Truly: A Cinderella Love Story
Yours Royally: A Cinderella Love Story

The "Kisses" series
Saltwater Kisses: A Billionaire Love Story
Kisses From Jack: The Other Side of Saltwater Kisses
Rainwater Kisses: A Billionaire Love Story
Champagne Kisses: A Timeless Love Story
Freshwater Kisses: A Billionaire Love Story
Sandcastle Kisses: A Billionaire Love Story
Hurricane Kisses: A Billionaire Love Story
Barefoot Kisses: A Billionaire Love Story
Sunrise Kisses: A Billionaire Love Story
Waterfall Kisses: A Billionaire Love Story
Island Kisses: A Billionaire Love Story

Other Novels
I Choose You: A Secret Billionaire Romance
His Every Desire: A Billionaire Seduction
Wolf Six's Salvation: A Shifter Love Story
Burned: A New Adult Love Story
Walking on Sunshine: A Sweet Summer Romance
An American Cinderella: A Royal Love Story
Mr. Darcy's Kiss: A Contemporary Pride and Prejudice